It was the

The crush of power. The crush of drugs. The crushing of emotions by the cocaine lure.

On the streets and in the nightclubs, men would meet and deal, a nervous exchange of currency for a small sample of heaven. At higher levels, men with eyes as cold and deadly as frozen steel would trade thick wads of bills for kidney-sized plastic bags of white death.

Carl Lyons wondered what it must be like to be a cop in Miami.

Hot blood, he thought. The tropics made for hot blood. Death in the afternoon, passion at night.

Carl Lyons felt the crush touch him.

Mack Bolan's

ABLE TEAM

ABLE TEAM

MIAMI CRUSH

Dick Stivers

A GOLD EAGLE BOOK FROM
W⊕RLDWIDE

TORONTO • NEW YORK • LONDON • PARIS
AMSTERDAM • STOCKHOLM • HAMBURG
ATHENS • MILAN • TOKYO • SYDNEY

First edition February 1987

ISBN 0-373-61228-1

Special thanks and acknowledgment to
Chuck Rogers for his contribution to this work.

Printed in Canada

PROLOGUE

San Diego, California, in the mid-1960s

"What is needed," Antonio "Tony" Pinto said to his wife, "is some way to hold them still while we work on them."

Carmen, his wife, listened in silence. Tony thought for several moments more, then muttered to himself, "Yes, that is what we need."

He stood with nearly all his weight on his left leg. That way he kept the pressure off the right hip, which had been shattered three years ago in an accident on board his tuna boat, the *Carmen*.

The boat bore his wife's name, and Tony Pinto loved them equally.

The Pintos were Portuguese and had emigrated from their homeland when they were both twenty-two to work in the rich agricultural areas of California's central valley, near Tulare. But the love of the sea had been too strong for Tony, something the fields and vineyards could not overcome. Finally the day came when they said goodbye to their relatives and friends and headed for the coast.

They ended up in San Diego. The booming tuna industry meant plenty of jobs for strong young men.

Such men were needed to work the boats, hauling the nets and handling the catch. It was backbreaking work, but there was money in it.

It could also be dangerous.

Tony Pinto wasn't afraid of hard work, and the hazards of the sea didn't intimidate him.

Carmen got a job in town, while he went out on the boats. And, when most of the fishermen claimed their wages—which they always underreported by half to their wives—and hit the town for sprees of big spending, drinking and fighting, Tony would go home to Carmen. The Pintos were blessed with children, and by the time they were thirty they had three sons and a daughter.

They lived frugally, and five years later they owned their own boat.

"The start of our fleet," Tony had announced proudly. "Our flagship, my *Carmen*."

His prediction proved to be true.

The "fleet" grew with his family. By the time he and Carmen were fifty, the one-boat "fleet" had become three. The Pintos had become prominent and prosperous in the San Diego tuna harvest. By then, Tony's sons did most of the actual sailing and fishing, but Tony insisted on going out on the boats whenever he could.

When they were fifty-two, fate hammered them a little. Tragedy struck. A hoist on the back of one of the boats, straining against the weight of the nets and the catch, buckled.

In one sense—though none of Tony's family could possibly have known it—that event may have marked the beginning of a trail.

The trail was one that would lead ultimately to a mission that would push the men of Able Team to the limit. Maybe a little beyond the limit. But only a time traveler or a fortune-teller—somebody able to see the future—could have known that, because the hoist buckled more than twenty years ago.

Able Team had not even been created.

Carl Lyons would have been in high school, playing football at Crescenta Valley High, near Glendale, just outside of Los Angeles.

Rosario Blancanales, already possessed of the winning smile and charm that would later earn his nickname "the Politician," would have been in basic training with the U.S. Army; next stop, airborne school and then Vietnam.

Hermann "Gadgets" Schwarz, just out of high school, would have been pursuing electronics and was probably beginning to realize that Vietnam was going to be next on his list of things to do, too. Even if he didn't put it there, his uncle—Uncle Sam, that is— would.

Still, a time traveler—someone able to look forward and backward along the time dimension—could see how things like this were connected. He would realize that the collapse of the tower was the first in a series of events that would someday involve the young Lyons and his partners.

Tony's youngest son, Miguel, saw the tower start to go.

The steel frame, the boom, that supported the arm that hoisted the nets twisted to one side. The sea was rough, and the boat squirreled sideways from the uneven pressure, causing Tony to lose his balance and fall under the collapsing rig.

"Papa!" Miguel shouted.

He was a stocky, strong young man, twenty-three years old. As the skeletal steel supports bent, then held, then bent some more, Miguel leaped forward on the small deck to save his father.

He almost made it.

Miguel seized one of Tony's arms and tried to drag him back from under the straining steel framework. The small boat pitched and jerked on the sea. Miguel struggled against the slippery surface of the deck, fighting to maintain his balance.

Then the rig tore completely loose.

The screech of tortured steel cut through the storm. The catch and net fell into the sea, where they struck with a tremendous foaming splash and sank out of sight. The steel tower whipped around and hit Tony in the right hip, shattering it into a mass of piercing bone fragments. The blow tore Tony free from Miguel's grip and knocked him across the deck.

Miguel lost his balance and fell onto the deck. He shook his head and pushed onto all fours, looking for his father.

"Papa!"

He scrambled forward on the pitching surface, trying to reach his injured parent. Tony's eyes were wide with shock, and his mouth worked convulsively.

Son found father just as the heavy boom fell to the deck.

It hit Miguel in the shoulders, breaking his neck and killing him instantly.

Tony and Carmen did not question God's judgment in taking their youngest son. These things were not for them to understand, they said. They buried Miguel with tearful dignity two weeks later. The funeral had been delayed so that Tony could be there, his lower body immobilized by the cast and his face gray with pain and grief.

Tony Pinto never again went out in the boats. The motion of the boat caused his hip too much pain, he said. He left it to his remaining two sons.

What he did do was open a ship-rigging yard—Pinto Steel and Shipfitting—in National City, just south of San Diego.

The yard started modestly, then grew steadily. They did ship repair work, welding, cutting, and sold steel of all types. But the first project Tony undertook when he opened the yard was to redesign the steel tower used to hoist the nets from the sea. He improved and ultimately began to manufacture the very device that had given way on the *Carmen* and had led to his son's death.

The Pintos saw it as a fitting memorial for Miguel.

A time traveler observing these events would make another note, marking this as the next link in the chain that stretched into the future.

The chain would inevitably lead to Able Team.

Tony's business did so well that he was able to install the steel structures "at cost" on any boat whose owner or captain ordered one. Pinto Steel and Shipfitting neither wanted nor received a profit on the towers.

"From Miguel," he would say.

The welding on the frames took a long time because they were so cumbersome. So it was that one day, watching the workmen, Tony realized they needed some way to hold the massive frame still while they wo.ked on it.

He gave it some thought. Finally, he hit on the idea of mounting a heavy industrial vise on the wall, a vise big enough to hold the basic frame of the hoist while the supports were added and the finishing welds performed. In the end, the vise didn't go on the wall. Instead, they mounted it to a heavy steel upright about six feet out from the wall.

The upright was a massive piece of I beam some seven or eight feet long. They secured it to the concrete floor by four heavy bolts. Another steel bar made a T at the top and ran to each side, parallel to the wall. Still other stringers, also made of steel, ran from each end of the T over to the wall.

The vise was a monster.

They mounted it to the upright I beam, about eye level, some five and a half feet off the ground. A thick steel shaft, or worm drive, controlled the jaws. The shaft had deep threads on it, which meshed with teeth on the base of the jaws. When the shaft rotated the jaws moved sideways, either being opened or closed by the worm drive.

Though the result couldn't actually compete with a General Motors assembly line, the process was speeded up considerably. Even a heavy steel frame could be clamped in the jaws of the massive vise and held immobile while the finishing welds were performed.

"Those frames won't be goin' anywhere when that baby is tightened down," Tony proclaimed with pride as he surveyed the finished product. "Not until we want 'em to."

His wife smiled. Her husband was a good man, she thought.

"Just don't get your head caught in there," he added, giving her a wink. "Give you a headache for sure."

Carmen knew that he was trying to shock her, a gentle teasing by the gruesome thought. She acknowledged it, making a sound of protest, then rested her hand lightly on his shoulder as they stood there.

They had been blessed with a good life. Even a bad thing like Miguel's death had brought good to the world, because now others would be spared his fate. Perhaps that was God's way the Pintos thought, that bad things should ultimately produce good.

If a time traveler possessed a sense of irony, he might note that the reverse might also be true. Maybe good things could produce bad, as well.

In twenty years or so, they would see.

1

The checker at the San Diego Super-Mart paused momentarily before she punched the Total key. She had fair skin with a dusting of freckles across her nose and cheekbones, light brown hair that was almost a coppery color and a 36D chest. A name tag pinned to the blue Super-Mart smock, on the upper slope of one of the *D*'s said "Karen."

It was nearly four in the afternoon. Karen had been working since the store opened at six that morning. She felt as tired as she looked.

"Will there by anything else?" Her right hand poised over the keys of the computerized cash register, like a bird of prey ready to strike on a small animal.

"No."

Mr. Personality, Karen thought.

Not "no, thank you." Or even "no, that's all." She hit the Total key. The machine did its thing, running the total and then displaying it in digits, as well as printing the figure on the cash register tape.

Karen read the amount aloud. "That will be $46.21 please."

The customer pulled a check from a pad inside his black vinyl checkbook cover. As the pen moved across the paper Karen read the name and address printed on the personalized form.

Allan Ball lived in Encinitas, a yuppie suburb of San Diego.

She looked at the customer.

Sallow complexion, brown hair. Wraparound sunglasses, which at the moment were stuck on the top of his head. Tall, maybe six-one, except that he walked with a slouch. It was as if he was trying to be cool, to affect a carefree grace. If that's what he was after, Karen thought, he had missed. Instead of achieving a casual look, it appeared that he had bad posture. His body curved like a single parenthesis.

Karen wondered if he used drugs. Cocaine.

Her brother was a cop, and she had heard him and his friends refer to Encinitas as the cocaine capital of California. Three C's, he called it.

Karen could believe it. Locally, Encinitas certainly had that reputation, from the consumer's perspective, at least. Hey, she thought, that's even better. Make it four C's: cocaine consumer's capital of California.

Tired though she was, Karen smiled at the thought.

It made sense, of course. Encinitas was located right above San Diego, which was fast becoming the Miami of the West Coast in terms of importation. And, according to her brother, *that* made sense, too—geographically, San Diego was comparable to Miami. It was the southernmost port and metropolitan area on the coast, accessible by air or boat.

And, ironically, the Feds contributed to San Diego's growing popularity in the cocaine business. In recent times the law enforcement efforts at the Florida end had intensified dramatically. And, when the pressure increased at the Florida end, it was only logical that the trade would begin to move to the West Coast.

Coke flows downhill or away from the heat, she thought.

"They won't even let you live in Encinitas unless you use coke," Mike had quipped just the other day, in fact. "It's a requirement, like you have to be a citizen to vote or be sixteen to get a driver's license."

"You're crazy," Karen had said, laughing.

She was half-drunk at the time, but thought it well to conceal the fact that she was not entirely unfamiliar with these matters herself.

"I mean it," he persisted, grinning. "Hell, they don't even talk like we do, all the same words have different meanings. They're so used to it, you can't even carry on a normal conversation with 'em."

"Like what?" she had asked.

"Drawing straws doesn't mean let's decide who has to do something. It means passing around drug paraphernalia.

"Hell, you try to write somebody a traffic ticket and tell them they crossed over the white line, and they freak out, thinking they must have dropped their stash. You go to a ball game, even, and somebody asks about the score—hell, everybody stops and listens, like that stockbroker commercial—they think you're talking about scoring some dope."

Karen regarded the customer on the other side of the counter with a critical eye. He had the look of somebody whose acquaintance with the white stuff was more than passing. Somebody on the down-slide, she thought.

He finished drawing the check and scrawled his name on the signature line. Allan Ball. Just like the printed name, she noted.

He had written it for $66.21. Twenty over the amount of the purchase.

Karen turned the check over. The reverse bore the machine printing that indicated the check had already been approved. The Super-Mart stores did this by a computerized machine called the Check Approval Center.

Karen liked the Check Approval Center. It meant she didn't have to get involved in asking for a driver's license and a major credit card, taking down the information and then getting that prick Ralph Lindley, the store manager, to approve the check. If the customer got the machine's okay, that was good enough. Less hassle, less thinking on Karen's part. And less contact with Lindley, who persisted in trying to pat her on the ass every time he got within three feet of her.

Guys like that never see past the tits, she thought. They were always hassling her, making comments about her body. Like he should talk—skinny wimp that he is. Karen had wondered about lodging a complaint against her boss, sexual harrassment, that sort of thing. But it would probably be washed out somewhere along the line; after all, it was her word against his.

Then she thought of the customer's name, Ball— boy, Lindley would have found some way to make a sexual reference to *that* if he had had to approve the check for her.

The Check Approval Center was the latest innovation at the Super-Mart stores. It did it all. No humans involved.

Of course, it had been a pain for the first few months, getting everybody signed up for the system and showing them how to use it. Karen had thought she would go nuts, having to explain it over and over until it became rote for her.

"See the blue balloons over there by aisle five? That's the Check Approval Center. Put your check into the machine, and stick in your Check Approval card, that blue one that looks like a credit card.

"The machine will ask you to punch in your code number, and then the computer will okay your check, and you can come to the checkstand."

Standard responses to the standard questions became rote, too.

"No, I'm sorry. You have to go to the Check Approval Center *first*, before you come to the checkout stand."

And, she went on, "No, I'm sorry. I can't do it the old way, even just this once. You'll have to go through the new procedure."

But as time went on, most of the customers adjusted to it, and the checkstands moved faster.

The code number prevented anybody who found or stole a wallet containing the check-approval credit card from being able to cash checks at Super-Mart. The card wouldn't work without the code number.

It made for a simple and effective system.

Of course, if the customer was dumb enough to write the code number down somewhere in that wallet, all bets were off. Not even the Super-Mart com-

puterized Check Approval Center could protect people
from their own stupidity.

Allan Ball—the real Allan Ball—had been that stupid.

He had actually written his code number on the
card, with a marking pen. And, as a result, the man at
the checkstand was committing his third felony that
day, forging Ball's name to the check, then passing it
to Karen.

"Uttering," it was called under California criminal
law, section 470 of the Penal Code, to be exact.

Karen's brother, the cop, had explained it to her.
The forger "uttered" a check, according to the law,
when he "offered it as genuine" to another person.

From force of habit Karen scanned the check to
make sure it was completed correctly. Date right. Nu-
meric amount matched the handwritten amount.
Signed. Then she turned it over and made sure the
machine had authorized the extra twenty.

It had.

She tore off the register tape and took the twenty out
of the cash drawer. Two tens.

"Ten, and twenty," she said automatically, putting
the bills into her customer's palm. "Thank you and
come again."

The sallow man with the slouch grunted something.

Jesus, thought Karen. The more she looked at this
guy, the worse he looked. Strung out. Hunted. Maybe
even haunted. Next stop, the basement, or worse.

Actually, she reflected, he looked scared. Scared to
death as a matter of fact.

Karen had no way of knowing how right she was.

The customer walked out of the store to where his car was parked. A red Porsche with personalized license plates—A BALL. It was "his car" in only a limited sense, the same way it was "his" checking account he had used to buy the food. Allan Ball didn't need either of them anymore.

Soon, neither would the man who had just come out of the Super-Mart.

He unlocked the Porsche and swung the plastic bags of groceries—mainly liquor—across to the passenger's seat. He had to bend over in order to lean into the low car.

As he stood up the fake Mr. Ball felt a blaze of pain in his skull.

He wondered if he had clobbered his head on the doorframe of the Porsche.

Another part of his mind knew better. They had caught up to him at last.

That's strange, he thought. The blow hadn't put him out immediately. They must have hit him with something that had some give to it, maybe a sand club. That would fit the pattern—Lalo, the Cuban, was a pro.

The pavement surged up toward him. Still, he retained almost ten percent of waking consciousness. Then, that, too, started slipping away. Walls of darkness pressed in on him from all sides like a vise, the black night of unconsciousness broken only by images that flashed through his mind.

It didn't matter anymore.

Nothing mattered now, not even life. No, he thought, that's not quite right. One thing still mattered. How long it would take him to die. And how much it would hurt.

That was Lalo—it had to be—and Lalo would make it hurt.

That's what they did to informants, and that's what he was. Not Allan Ball or any of the other three or four identities he had used over the past few weeks when he'd been on the run. No, he was Danny Forbes, originally from Los Angeles but most lately from Miami, Florida.

Fast Danny, he was called. John and Edna Forbeses' oldest son Daniel. Born and raised in Los Angeles, California. Known to the LAPD since he was fifteen years old.

He carried other labels, as well. It depended on who was describing him.

Snitch. Rat. A turncoat. State's evidence. A rollover. A protected witness.

The letter had been his last hope. If anybody could save him, it was Carl Lyons. Lyons, the former L.A. cop who had gone off and joined the Feds. Lyons, who had gotten him by the balls on that big coke caper—when was it? Hell, it seemed like a lifetime ago.

Lyons, the Ironman, had convinced him that being an informant was lousy, all right. Still, it was better than prison by a thousand miles.

"All you do is make the buys," the Ironman had said, when he had explained it to him. "We'll take it from there."

"Stick it up your ass," Danny had retorted. "I've been around. I know how it works. You can't make the case unless I testify, and then I'm dead meat."

Lyons shook his head.

"It's not like that these days. I won't try to prosecute the sale. I'll just wait a week, then I'll get a search warrant for the guy's place. Your name won't even appear in the warrant. Nobody'll ever know it was you who made the buy that led to the warrant."

And that was how it started.

Lyons had proved to be as good as his word. He had always treated Danny fair and square, even if Forbes was a crook.

But time marches on. Nothing is forever. Things change. Lyons had finally gone on to other things. He left the Justice Department and went to something else. Danny didn't know exactly where, but he thought Lyons was still with the government. Danny had been handed off to the FBI some years back. He continued his roll as an informant, making cases for the Major Narcotics Division.

Somehow, Lalo had figured it out.

Lalo, the thin-faced Cuban killer, was only a kid when Castro took over. However, he had been a murderous criminal even then. Now, Lalo was the chief enforcer and torturer for Ramon Lucero, the man who controlled the flow of cocaine in and out of Miami.

Lucero's ass was in a legal sling now. He was coming up for trial on a major drug conspiracy and racketeering case, being prosecuted under the RICO law, the legal acronym for the Racketeer Influenced and Corrupt Organizations statute.

Thanks in large part to the work of Danny Forbes.

Of course, Lucero wasn't actually in jail, in custody. Some soft federal judge had allowed him to post bail of a million dollars—pocket change for Lucero—and had let him out. Hell, some of the import deals Lucero financed were worth more than that.

The word hit the streets. "Get Fast Danny."

Lalo was the field commander of Lucero's private army of professional killers. Originally, most of them had been the dregs of Cuban prisons, who came to America thanks to a policy under the Carter administration.

Only a man, or animal, like Lalo could control those bastards, and there was only one way even he could do it.

Be worse than the worst of them.

He would laugh as he sliced off genitals and then watched the blood stream out. Later, when the fun was over, the interrogation and punishment complete, the laughter became a thin, mean smile. Then it was that Lalo would slide the blade into the guts of his helpless victim and slowly, almost lovingly, move it around in the warm wet viscera.

Killing was personal to Lalo.

The initial torture might be fun, but the finality of ending the life gave him a particular intimacy with his victim, one that was special and private.

He liked it.

Even his men were afraid of him. Lalo could do anything.

Lalo had gotten through the shield of the witness protection program, the supposedly *impenetrable* informant safety operation run by the U.S. Justice Department. For six weeks now, Danny Forbes had been on the run. And all the while, Lalo was behind him, leaving a trail of pain and death as he followed the scent.

Closing the gap.

With nowhere to turn, Forbes had written a letter to Lyons. He sent it care of the Justice Department, hoping it would somehow be forwarded to the rugged ex-cop.

Lyons was his last chance.

Maybe nobody could stop Lalo and his heavily armed band of killers. The man was the closest thing to pure evil on this earth. Maybe he was the devil incarnate, Lucifer up from hell to walk among men.

But if anybody could stop Lalo, it was Lyons, the Ironman himself.

The letter had bombed.

It must have. If Lyons were going to come, he'd have done so by now.

Of course, Danny knew Lyons didn't owe him anything. Hell, even if the letter got to him, there was nothing to guarantee that he would try to help.

But for some reason, that didn't seem likely. Danny somehow felt that Lyons would try to help if he could.

He was just that kind of guy. Tough. Ruthless, when he had to be. But underneath it, he had a strange compassion for those less fortunate than himself, and an understanding that nobody was perfect.

As tough as Lalo, even. Maybe. But without the twisted meanness, the twisted psychopathy that made Lalo so evil.

"I don't expect you to be a goddamn angel," Lyons had told him. That struck Danny as funny, using "goddamn" in connection with "angel."

The conversation had taken place in a holding cell somewhere in Los Angeles. Lyons had arrested Danny and could make it stick. Usually Danny didn't worry about arrests, but he was still on probation, and his last judge had been a bastard. The sad truth for Danny was that this guy Lyons had him by the short hairs. His only chance was to become a CI, or confidential informant, somebody who passed information to the authorities.

"I don't expect you to like me," the Ironman had continued. "I only expect one thing."

"What's that?" Fast Danny had asked sullenly.

"I expect you to understand this. Listen, and listen good. You play square with me, and I'll play square with you. You'll get good money if you turn good cases. I'll protect you as best I can."

"So?"

"So, this. If you hold back on me, if I catch you dealing drugs behind my back, if you fuck me over in any way, the joint will be Sunday school compared to what I'll do to you."

"I don't give a shit about the joint, Goldilocks," he had snarled back. "Prison is a cakewalk compared to what those guys will do to me if they catch me ratting on them."

Then he had discovered a strange thing. It was a new experience, actually.

He found out what it felt like to be pinned against the wall with his feet eight inches off the floor, held up by the hand—*one* hand—that was clamped around his throat like a steel band. He dangled there, looking down into the grim face of the psycho they called the Ironman.

"Don't call me Goldilocks," Lyons said softly.

Danny had tried to say he wouldn't call Lyons that any more. Ever again. Honest. Cross his heart. He tried to apologize. But he couldn't because of the pressure around his throat. So he just bobbed his head frantically, as much as he could bob it, given the fact that his head and neck were held against the wall.

"You worried about what they'll do to you? The crooks?"

Danny didn't answer.

"Well, *that* will be Sunday school, too, compared to what I'll do if you fuck me over."

Danny believed him. Something about that face inspired belief. Something about . . . the eyes. That was it. The eyes made a believer out of him.

They were grim eyes. Blue, but cold. Eyes that couldn't be lied to. Eyes that said, believe, or else.

After what seemed like a very long time, Lyons let him down. He set him back on his feet, then released his throat. Danny's legs went out from under him, and he crumpled into a sitting position on the floor.

So Danny had signed on. And now he was dying because of it.

He didn't blame Lyons. Hell, Danny knew he was a big boy, and he'd probably have been in prison by now, or more likely dead, if he hadn't gone to work for the Ironman.

The last of his darkening consciousness began to ebb away as the walls of blackness pressed in on him. It felt like some great black vise tightening down on him, and Danny knew he was going to die.

So the letter had bombed. Or maybe Lyons wasn't even with the government any longer. Hell, maybe he wasn't even alive.

No matter. It was over now. Or it would be after his mind exploded from the pain he knew lay ahead.

The images faded as the blackness took him down.

2

National City police officer Gary McMurray wheeled his black-and-white police car into the alley near the waterfront.

The early morning sun fought to penetrate the coastal fog. The sun would finally prevail—summer was fast approaching, and the day promised to be a hot one. And then, the night fog would come back and the struggle would begin again, the contest never over, neither side emerging victorious.

The immediate effect of the battle was a pale gray light that washed over the area.

"Mac," as his friends called him, had always thought that the never-ending give-and-take of the fog and the sun was in some ways like life itself. It was certainly like fighting crime in the streets—you never really won. Sometimes it looked like you were making progress, sometimes you lost ground. The only thing that never changed was the fact that the struggle would always be there.

Not losing was the best thing to hope for.

Maybe that was what winning meant. On the streets, anyway. But "not losing" was at best only temporary. Someday, inevitably, he would lose the big one.

Then they would stick him in a box, stick the box in a hole and cover it up.

He wondered who would be "Unit 224 Alpha" when that happened. One thing was certain—*somebody* would be. Like a massive old ship, the world would keep going after they jettisoned his carcass.

Dilapidated warehouses, most of them empty and abandoned, squatted desolately on either side of the alley. They had a hostile look about them, a sort of defiant anger at being cast aside.

Mac's uniform was brand-new. He had just come out of a stint in the detective bureau, and his old patrol uniforms had been made obsolete when the department opted for navy instead of the khaki that most San Diego-area police agencies wore.

He liked the blue better. Sharper, somehow. More businesslike. And on the practical side, it didn't show the blood and dirt like the tan did. The new uniform was a fitting token of his return to patrol. Though he would miss being a detective, he also enjoyed being the first man on the scene.

It was all police work.

His eyes probed the aging structures on each side as the police unit idled down the alley. The tires made tiny popping sounds as they crunched gravel and small rocks against the pitted pavement.

His body reminded him that it was time for his six-o'clock nature call. He knew it wasn't likely that there was anybody around this desolate, godforsaken part of town to be offended if he ignored the formalities of finding a rest room.

The deserted, falling-down warehouse provided just the place.

Originally, it had been a ship-fitting yard. Today it looked like part of a futuristic ghost town.

Half of one brick wall had tumbled into a pile of rubble. The roof sagged. High along the face of the structure, faded and dirty white letters proclaimed Pinto Steel and Shipfitting. Two huge windows, one on each side of the entrance, the glass long since gone, returned Mac's probing gaze with an impassiveness that somehow made his skin crawl.

McMurray relieved himself against the wall. Watch out for flying concrete chips, he thought, we're talking high pressure all the way.

A long, low, deathlike groan rolled through the fog.

Mac was instantly on full alert.

It was impossible to tell where it came from or even if it were man or animal that made it. He strained his ears and probed the mist with his eyes.

Nothing moved. No sounds reached his ears.

Yet something was there.

Mac had been a cop for some ten years. Before that he had done a double hitch in the Marines, first in Vietnam, and later on, embassy duty. He hadn't survived that long by ignoring his sixth sense.

He crouched and moved quickly back to the car. Reaching inside, it was only a matter of seconds until he had the Remington pump shotgun in hand.

Handy-talkie turned to "mute," no keys jangling on his leather gear, he moved forward.

Pinto Steel and Shipfitting loomed before him. He decided to check it out first.

The shotgun was a comforting weight in his grip. McMurray knew that it was a vastly superior weapon to the service revolver, and it never ceased to amaze him that more officers didn't take their shotguns into potentially violent situations. Hell, half of them bitched about having to wear the lightweight body armor the department issued.

Of course, a lot of times it wasn't feasible to carry the shotgun. It was longer and more awkward. Sometimes, if the risk of a firefight was minimal, it meant more to have the hands free, unencumbered by a long gun. And, a lot of police departments got nervous about taking out the shotguns for PR—public relations—purposes.

Well, PR didn't matter here. This wasn't the crowded streets of a city. Nobody would see him.

Besides, it wasn't likely that he would need his hands free.

And, finally, he realized that although this was probably nothing, with the chances of gunfire remote, he might as well be prepared. Only one chance in a million of getting your ass eaten by a lion at city hall, but once is enough.

The warehouse stood before him in the hazy gray light.

His sixth sense—hell, the seventh and eighth ones as well—screamed at him. Something was definitely up. Though his body functioned automatically to locate and evaluate cover and concealment, part of his mind couldn't help wondering what some unsympathetic judge on the Supreme Court would do with this.

"You see, Your Honor, I was just chipping bricks off the side of this old building when I heard this noise."

"Could you be more specific, Officer McMurray?"

"Well, I was taking a leak, and I heard this weird sound."

"What sort of weird sound, Officer?"

"Like a groan or something. It made the hair on the back of my neck stand up."

"So, Officer, you went and got your shotgun because the hair on your neck stood up while you were, er, uh, relieving yourself. Is that it? I see.... No, no further questions, thank you...."

To hell with them. You had to have priorities. Survival first. Protect lives and property second. Making a case that satisfied the Ivy League, ivory tower justs came in a distant third.

Quickly he slipped forward and flattened himself against the wall a few feet to the left of the cavernous entrance. Unconsciously he checked himself—shotgun in port arms position, left hand on the knurled wood grip to the pump slide, right hand on the pistol grip, right index finger on the trigger, safety off.

And another thing—a biggie—his fly zipped. The papers would have a field day if he got himself wasted with his pants unzipped and his, uh, unit hanging out.

McMurray eased forward, his back to the wall, leading with his left shoulder. Near the edge of the door he stopped and listened.

The vague roar of freeway noise made its way through the gray fog. Somewhere an alley cat yowled in feline lust. Heavy metal banged as a garbage truck, probably a couple of blocks away, raised a dumpster overhead.

Nothing too sinister in all that, he thought, unless the imagination was allowed to run wild.

Another noise reached him, this one much closer, more immediate. It was a snapping sound, the noise that a sapling makes when it has been bent until it finally cracks. For reasons he couldn't identify a chill ran down his back, and the hairs on his arms stood up.

The sound came from inside the structure.

Metal squeaked, the protesting noise of reluctant machinery being turned. Whatever it is, it needs oil, he thought idiotically. Then the popping sound came again.

His ears were hypersensitive. The freeway sounds receded into the distance, his brain filtering them out so that he could concentrate on nearby matters. The low tones of voices reached him, then a brief glint of white light.

Silently he crouched to peer around the doorframe. The crouching was a standard officer survival technique: if a hostile had a gun trained on the doorframe, chances were it would be at head height rather than lower.

The gray light illuminated the interior of the building. On the far side stood three men, their backs to him, facing a vertical steel pole.

One of the men had a machine pistol, an Uzi or some similar weapon, thought Mac. He held it carelessly, the weapon supported by a strap over his shoulder, right hand loosely on the grip. A second man had something dark in his hands; it didn't look like a weapon by the way the man was holding it.

Then McMurray realized it was a camera.

The third man, evidently the leader, stood back from the other two. He smoked a dark cigarette or thin cigar. He was lean and brown. Hard, sinewy muscles twisted along the length of his arms; webs of prominent veins played along their surfaces. Other knots of muscles showed beneath the shoulders of his shirt.

Even at that distance he was an evil-looking bastard.

Belatedly Mac saw the fourth man.

He stood behind and to one side of the upright post, facing the others and looking in Mac's direction.

The fourth man's arms moved—Mac couldn't see exactly how, or what he was doing—and again McMurray heard the squeaking noise and the snapping sound of a breaking sapling.

"Bueno pues. Cuidado. No haces tan rápido." Loosely translated, it meant, "Okay. Be careful. Don't go too fast." Mac wrinkled his brow; the men must be Cuban he thought.

But what was he referring to?

The command came from the leader. The squeaking stopped, and the man with the camera stepped to one side, as if to get a better snapshot. As he did, Mac was able to see the answer to his question.

And in that instant he knew it was a sight he would never forget.

The scene before him would be frozen in the rooms of his brain forever. And though he couldn't know it then, it would come back to him in nightmares for years to come.

His mind worked on several levels. For some strange reason the rational part of his mind recalled the principles he had learned about how the eye sees things. Light strikes an object and is reflected. The eye picks it up; the brain interprets the images.

All very neat and scientific, except that the goddamn brain is too vivid.

It was a man. Or, to be more precise, what used to be a man.

He was hanging in front of the pole. But no rope encircled his neck. No meat hook was thrust into his back, a favorite of big-city mobsters back east.

He was held there by the jaws of a massive vise that was mounted on the pole.

And clamped on either side of his skull.

Mac's brain took in the data and analyzed it with a terrible clarity. The man was naked. A dark red hole gaped where the genitals had been. The blood pooled in an irregular black shape on the dirty cement floor. The jaws of the vise, one on each side of the face, had been closed until they were about four inches apart.

The eyes bulged white and hideous from the distorted features. The lower jaw was crunched into an angle, one side higher than the other. The forehead protruded under the pressure.

McMurray knew what the sapling snapping sound had been. With vivid clarity his imagination visualized the tough bone of the skull stubbornly resisting the inexorable pressure of the vise, until the pressure got too great and...

The man with a camera took another picture as the leader calmly smoked his thin cigar.

Training and duty took over. Still crouched to peer around the doorframe, he made a light shift into a shooter's kneeling position. With his left foot planted flat, knee up, and right knee and toe on the cement, McMurray eased the shotgun around the doorframe.

Then he had the dreadful tableau in his vision over the barrel of the shotgun, and it was time.

"Freeze! Police officer!" He screamed the command, shotgun ready. If they didn't understand English, maybe they'd understand Remington.

The four men showed they had been trained in combat skills. They didn't hesitate an instant. Instead they scattered, diving in opposite directions as the man with the Uzi swung around with a well-directed spray of gunfire in Mac's direction.

The fast, sharp cracks of the 9 mm weapon echoed throughout the warehouse, an insistent hammering as the weapon sprayed slugs toward the entrance, where McMurray was crouched. Ricochets sang away into the distance, and splinters of lead and cement peppered the walls.

Mac fired once, twice, a third time.

The shotgun made heavy, authoritative booms compared to the crackling fire of the Uzi.

The shotgun blasts were evenly spaced but quick. The spacing came from the rhythmic clack-clack as he worked the slide of the pump shotgun between each blast, first pulling it toward him, then slamming it forward. The empty brass and plastic casing flipped to the right and back as the extractor did its job, then the breach closed on a new round. All the while his mind absorbed the data from his eyes, correlated it with his training and directed the shots.

He felt no fear—there wasn't time. All three shots took maybe two seconds, a quick "Boom! Clack-clack, boom! Clack-clack, boom!"

McMurray carried four rounds of double 0 buckshot in the pump. Each double 0 pellet was equivalent to a .32-caliber bullet, and there were nine pellets per round.

He knew what that could do.

The man with the machine pistol staggered backward, as though struck in the chest by a sledgehammer; in a sense, thought Mac, that was what had actually happened. The man's dying nerves caused his fingers to clamp around the grip and trigger of the weapon, and the staccatto burst continued for a moment longer, though the rounds sprayed off to one side, unaimed.

Mac directed the second shot at the leader, who had sprinted toward the back of the building with unbelievable speed. It was almost as if he had dematerialized, and the word "ninja" came to McMurray's mind, a Cuban ninja.

Even as he fired the second one, McMurray knew it had missed.

Instinctively he also knew not to waste another on the leader. The guy was gone, and the immediate threat came from elsewhere.

The veteran officer sensed how close he was to being killed. Moreover, he also somehow knew which of the other two men had the weapon and where he was located. Combat training and experience kicked in— neutralize the most dangerous weapon first.

Try explaining *that* to a judge or jury, he thought. No way, unless they had combat experience, too.

The third round from the shotgun caught the Cuban at the base of the throat, where his neck joined his upper chest. The shot was a little higher than ideal, Mac thought crazily, because he had been trained to shoot for the center of mass, to stop the attack, and that was the torso. But what the hell, it did the trick, got the job done, so to speak.

The load of double 0 all but decapitated the man.

Besides, as he thought later, this coconut bandit was a short little bastard, and McMurray was used to taller targets.

As suddenly as it had begun, it was over. The warehouse echoed from the gunfire. The acrid smell of cordite drifted back over the crouching officer.

A car roared to life behind the warehouse. The sound was followed almost instantly by the screech of tires, and McMurray knew that the leader and the fourth Cuban had rabbited. They were history as far as he was concerned.

His movements were guided by the training he had received, first in Vietnam and later as a cop. McMurray did not spring after the car. Instead he remained in his kneeling stance behind the cover of the doorframe, the pump shotgun at his shoulder, while he checked the interior of the warehouse.

There just could be another Cuban. Just because it was two down and two had escaped out the back didn't mean that was all there had been.

His eyes scanned the cavernous building, probing the interior in the steel-gray morning light.

Nothing.

Still crouching behind his cover, McMurray lowered the shotgun from his shoulder, butt down, muzzle up. Then he reached for the two extra shotgun rounds he kept tucked behind his speedloaders, under his belt. He fed the three new rounds into the weapon's tubular magazine by feel, never taking his eyes off the scene before him.

Still nothing.

No new enemy, no movement from the previous ones.

Only then did he rise and move forward. Only then did he become aware of the blood roaring in his ears, of the pounding of his heart. He wiped the sweat from his brow with the back of his left hand. It came away red, and he knew a fragment of bullet or cement must have stung him. He rubbed the back and then the front of his hand on the leg of his uniform trousers as he tried to wipe away the blood on one side and the sweat on the other.

The clang of metal on cement came from behind him.

McMurray dropped to a crouch and pivoted, throwing the shotgun to his shoulder in a single movement. Then his eyes found the source of the sound, and he caught himself a fraction of a second before blowing away an alley cat that streaked away from a pile of junk. The can it had knocked over still rolled back and forth on the cement floor.

He wheeled back, as though one of the dead men was attacking him, using the cat as a distraction. He had a sudden, terrible vision of the corpse lurching to feet that no longer worked and staggering forward, dead eyes glazed over but the body indestructible, unstoppable.

The bodies hadn't moved.

Somehow the incident served to break the tension. McMurray relaxed and actually smiled to himself. "Easy, pal," he said aloud. "Be cool, buddy," he added, then grinned again.

Still he walked over to the bodies sprawled on the cement floor and checked them. No threat there he thought, not in this life, anyway.

So much for the two Cubans, McMurray thought, but what about the other one, the pitiful bastard who had been the object of their attention. He looked at the ghastly form held upright by the monster clamp on its head and saw two bullet wounds that he didn't think had been there before.

They had probably come from the random spray from the dead Cuban's Uzi, he realized. Moreover, they weren't bleeding, not the way a live body bleeds; they were just oozing a little dark red. That only helped confirm what he already knew, which was that the man in the vise was far beyond help.

He took inventory.

One cop with sweaty palms, but alive.

One alley cat who had come to within about two seconds of being vaporized by a load of double 0, but alive.

Three dead men, two horizontal like dead men should be, and one vertical, which is how live men should be.

Welcome to National City, he thought.

National City "Vise."

3

"All rise!"

The bailiff's stentorian voice seemed to fill the courtroom. Feet shuffled and bumped as the audience of cops, lawyers, litigants, witnesses and spectators complied with the command.

The uninitiated—mainly crime victims and civilian witnesses in court for only their first or second time—looked startled and jerked to their feet as though important consequences followed the exercise. They waited and watched with something akin to awe for the formality of the law to be visited upon them. Finally they were rewarded as a silver-haired figure wearing a flowing black robe swept majestically into the courtroom from a door to one side of the bench.

Most of those present—the cops, the attorneys and most of the crooks—were more complacent about the whole business.

The complacent ones had seen it all before, especially the defendants, many of whom had more exposure to courtroom procedures than did their attorneys.

The bailiff continued his proclamation

"Department 27 of the Superior Court of the State of California is now in session, the Honorable A.

Donald Mayer presiding. Please be seated and come to order.''

Once again chairs squeaked and feet shuffled as the ''all rise'' scenario was run in reverse. A suitable pause followed. Then the court clerk, an attractive woman in her forties, reached for the top file of a pile on one corner of her desk.

She glanced at the tab along one edge of the folder and announced, ''Case number one on calendar, the people of the State of California versus Daniel Edwards, on for probation hearing and sentencing.''

In legal jargon, she was ''calling the calendar,'' reading off each case on the docket that morning.

Except for the newcomers to the system and the parties involved in the particular case, the audience settled back in their chairs. A sort of passive resignation, a collective ''oh, well'' descended over them as they prepared to wait until their own cases were called.

Among them was a rugged blond man dressed in designer jeans and an off-white shirt made of some sort of textured material. He sat in the back of the courtroom on the right-hand side, in the area traditionally occupied by law enforcement witnesses: the deputy sheriffs, police officers and detectives.

His name was Carl Lyons. He happened to be one of the most dangerous men in the world.

These days, not many people knew him, or even knew that he was alive. The nature of his work made it difficult for him to have many friends. It was simply too dangerous; there was too much chance that security would be compromised. Put another way, the shotgun blast fired at the falcon might also bring down whatever other birds—no matter how innocent—that were nearby and happened to stray into the pattern.

It had happened before, and a lovely young woman had died as a result.

Before he'd become what he was today—one of the world's best counterterrorist agents—Lyons had lived a "normal" life. That meant friends and acquaintances, barbecues, an occasional beer bust or swim party, and all the other trappings of a middle-class existence in Los Angeles.

Then he joined the Los Angeles Police Department.

The "normal" life was still there, but it had changed a little.

He began to look at the world differently. He started thinking in terms of crimes and lies, danger and death. Almost everybody had an angle, and a lot of the angles were illegal. Worse than that, they usually meant somebody was going to get hurt, that a strong one was going to take a bite out of a weak one.

That bothered him more than anything—the bullies, the greedy animals to whom "might was right."

"Somebody has to stick up for the underdogs," he once observed. "The reason we have cops is not to protect the rich and powerful, but to protect the ordinary guys who can't do it themselves."

Lyons became consumed with life in the police department. It provided a regular "fix" of danger, as well as a certain "us against the enemy" attitude. As time went on, his circle of friends narrowed a little.

Then came the day when somebody in the U.S. Justice Department recognized that Lyons was just the kind of man they were looking for. "Main Justice," as the agency headquarters was called by those on familiar terms with it, had gotten the go-ahead to create a special organized-crime and narcotics strike force.

Was Lyons interested, they asked.

Doing what, he had inquired.

The man from Main Justice put it simply: the strike force would target criminals not crimes. Instead of waiting for a crime to happen and then trying to solve it, they would go after the offenders in their native habitat.

Lyons liked that.

Being a street cop had taught him that the big fish, the ones who called the plays, were slippery. The strike force looked like a chance to set that right. So the blond law enforcement officer put aside the blue uniform and the black-and-white police car. The visible cop became the invisible cop, a hunter of sorts.

The circle of friends narrowed some more.

The Stony Man concept actually referred to two things. On a general level, it meant the antiterrorist efforts resulting from the leadership of Mack Bolan and his chief of operations, Hal Brognola.

In more concrete terms, Stony Man referred to the farm itself, a secret facility in Virginia that Lyons and the others knew as their home base.

The Stony Man Doctrine involved some of the same ends as the federal strike force. The means of achieving those ends, however, differed substantially.

The ends were the protection—hell, in some cases the very survival—of a way of life and the saving of individual lives threatened by organized criminal or terrorist actions. The means, though, involved bullets instead of laws, "ordnance instead of ordinances," in a sense. "Him or me" replaced constitutional rights, survival instead of due process.

Lyons quickly learned what this meant in real life.

It meant being one of the guys poised outside a door to some building or room. A guy who knew that beyond the door somewhere would be a group of terrorists. Usually the terrorists had hostages; usually they were well trained; always, they were heavily armed.

The door was right there, always in front of him. Waiting. Beyond it lay one hell of a good chance for death.

Lyons knew that at any moment he would be going through that door, hard and fast and tricky, searching for his target and waiting for the impact of the bullets, wondering if he would be hit and if he could keep going anyway.

How would it feel? Would it knock him down?

Would it hurt?

And Lyons would tell himself, *will* himself, to stay on his feet, no matter how hard he got it, so that maybe he could take a couple more of the bastards down before his own lights went out and he subsided onto the bright crimson smears that leaked out of him.

Would his life really flash before his eyes in that final second or two?

Lyons remembered that scientists believed the brain and nervous system worked by tiny electrical impulses that carried the messages to and from the brain. When the bullets struck, he wondered what the final messages from his brain would be. An instant replay of his entire life, all the events that had been stored somewhere in the biological "rooms" of his mind?

He had heard, and believed, that this would be possible. Every single thing a person experienced— every piece of "sensory data," as his Able Team partner Hermann "Gadgets" Schwarz put it—was retained by the memory. It was back there in the brain somewhere, available if only it could be found and recalled.

Or would those last messages be of something else, a flash of unbearable pain as the nerve-circuits overloaded, then finally blew like fuses in the old house his parents lived in? Perhaps fear? Panic?

"Oh, God, no! Not me! I don't want to die...".

Or maybe it woudn't be anything so dramatic.

Maybe the lights just went out, quietly, without fanfare. Hell, maybe a sense of peace, "free at last," to quote the old spiritual hymn.

Lyons learned quickly there was only one way to get the job done. It required turning off the logical mind so he could make that heart-stopping charge into the waiting guns. In a sense, that typified his way of living. Someday, he knew, it would do the same for his way of dying.

"Just nut up and do it."

Somebody, a member of the FBI's Special Weapons Squad, had once asked him what the "nut up" part meant.

"'Nut' as in crazy? 'Nut up' meaning go wacкo? Nuts? Or 'nut' as in balls, guts, that sort of thing?"

The Special Weapons man had good reason to be asking. He had just witnessed Lyons make a low, fast-diving entry through a door on a "high-risk" warrant. The Able Team man had gone in under the shotgun blast and, when his own weapon became disabled, had yanked the defender's ankles out from under him and then broken the man's neck in a single quick snap, using only his bare hands.

Lyons considered the question.

"I don't know," he finally responded. "I guess I never really thought about it."

The FBI man looked at him carefully, as if he had never seen a specimen like that before.

Maybe it was the sudden, swift finality of the neck-breaking—punctuated by the audible crack of bone as the vertebrae gave way—that made the Fed so nervous. His face wore a peculiar sort of uncertainty. It was the same look one might give a killer grizzly when the animal experts said, "Don't worry, that's a good tranquilizer. He's as harmless as a kitten right now."

The look said bullshit.

The look said this guy is the most dangerous animal he'd ever seen and there's no way the grizzly would ever be harmless unless he was dead with his head cut off. And maybe a stake through his heart, for good measure.

Lyons gave the question some more thought.

"It's a little bit of both, I guess. Crazy, sure. A little berserk helps in the right kind of fighting. But it's more than that. It's mainly guts. Balls. *Huevos rancheros.* Brass. Heart. Hell, I don't know. Just nut up and do it."

With the move to Stony Man Farm, the metamorphosis of Carl Lyons was complete.

"Died after a long illness" was the stock phrase newspapers used in the obituaries. Lyons realized that in a sense it applied to him. The ordinary man—former high school jock, tailgate parties at the ball games, go home to his wife and, someday, kids—was no more. The wife was gone; the kids would never happen.

C'est la vie. That's life.

Nor could the old Lyons ever exist again. Though not irreversible, Lyons's decision to go with the Stony Man Farm operation signaled the end of one life and the beginning of another.

Deceased. Buried. Forgotten.

This kind of work didn't encourage friends. Virtually the only people who knew Lyons was alive these days were his partners in the Stony Man operation. He had become one of those "say, whatever happened to him, anyway, you ever hear what he's doing these days" people.

Requiescat in pace, Carl Lyons.

Rest in peace.

The new Lyons was a different animal.

These days his weight hovered around one-ninety, up from what he had been as a cop, but down ten or fifteen from last year, when he had been hitting the weights five days a week. He still wore his blond hair short, as he had done even when it hadn't been fashionable.

The eyes had a special quality to them. "Blue ice," a woman had called them. "But tired," she added, kissing the creases in the corners. "Tired eyes."

The eyes of a killer, she might have added, had she known what a killer's eyes looked like.

Because when the job demanded it, Lyons was a killer.

The worst.

The best of the worst.

4

On this day, however, Lyons looked pretty much like any other witness in Judge Mayer's courtroom. And, like the other veterans of the judicial system, he settled back to wait.

Lyons also knew Judge Mayer. Because of this, he didn't hold out much hope that any real justice would occur. Or if it did, it would be by accident.

Also, this particular judge was the reason Lyons was there in the first place.

It didn't make sense, actually. Hal Brognola, chief of operations at Stony Man Farm, had asked him to check up on Judge Mayer. "Asked" was putting it mildly; "directed" would be more like it.

Just look in on him, Brognola had said.

Just see if he's still alive, still being a judge, still screwing over the cops, especially on narcotics cases.

"Why, Chief?" Lyons inquired. "We down to assassinating judges we don't like? That's a little heavy even for me."

Brognola's reply had been cool. "When you have a need to know, I'll tell you. Until then, just do it."

What the Stony Man chief was really saying, both by his words and his tone of voice, was that something was cooking that might involve this judge and that Lyons should scope him out and report.

It also meant, to Lyons, that something was up. A mission was in the offing.

High time.

He felt restless. Irritable. Aimless. "Custer looking for his last stand, Horatius looking for his bridge." He caught himself and mentally wrenched his thoughts away from those memories.

The lady who had said those words was dead, and would stay dead.

She had died because of Carl Lyons. Because she knew him. Whoa, Ironman, he said to himself, better stay away from thinking about that. That kind of guilt sucks.

Clearly, Brognola hadn't appreciated Lyons's question about why he was supposed to check up on the judge. His reply had contained a stronger message than just the words. Do your job, it had said, and I'll do mine. Don't ask questions.

Aloud, the Stony Man chief had continued, "Just see if he's still in business, sitting on the bench. Watch him for a couple of hours. Listen to his voice. Get a feel for the guy. Then report back."

"Sure, Chief," Lyons had said with a shrug, forgetting that Brognola couldn't see it over the telephone. "I'll let you know."

Now, in the courtroom, Lyons settled back to wait and watch.

The clerk would go through the cases one at a time, item by item, each time awaiting the judge's decision. Some would be sentencings. Some would be "motions," specific requests that the court make some order or another having to do with the case in question. There might be a "change of plea" or two, cases where the defense attorney and the prosecutor had struck a deal and the crook was ready to plead guilty. And maybe one or two cases would even be sent out to another courtroom for a jury trial.

Almost as if doing trials—letting a jury decide guilt or innocence—might even be one of the reasons the courts and judges were there.

Carl Lyons was not the only one in the courtroom who was dismayed by the prospect of a lengthy calendar or docket. From his own vantage point behind the raised bench, Judge Mayer himself surveyed the assemblage.

A single emotion beset the black-robed jurist.

Contempt.

He hated the prospect of having to do the job the taxpayers overpaid him to do. And he responded by displaying the singular arrogance and rudeness that had become his trademark on the bench.

He berated the attorneys.

Neither side was immune to his criticism. Usually, though, the prosecution got it worse than the defense. This may have had something to do with the fact that Judge Mayer was himself a former defense attorney, as well as a card-carrying member of the American Civil Liberties Union. Still, by and large, his rudeness tended to be universal.

He lambasted the police.

No investigation was good enough for Judge A. Donald Mayer. He could always find fault with some minute point of procedure. If possible, he would throw out the case. Unfortunately, at least so he thought, the police did a solid, sound investigation more often than not. In those cases, Judge Mayer resorted to simply criticizing anything he could think of, down to the punctuation in their reports.

He criticized the law.

Judge Mayer was actually a staunch supporter of the procriminal, antivictim policies of the California Supreme Court. He made liberal use of their case precedents to throw out cases that came before him. In so doing, of course, he paid strong lip service to the notion that the court's rulings were unduly liberal and favored the criminal.

In most cases, his rulings had to do with the so-called "exclusionary rule," which allows a judge to throw out any evidence obtained by the police if all the *i*'s weren't dotted or the *t*'s crossed.

And dotted or crossed *properly*, to boot.

"Properly," of course, was defined by the appellate courts, men and women who had never been inside a police car or had tried to break up a bar fight. Most of all, they had never been victims of any crimes themselves.

Most crimes didn't occur in areas where the judges lived. Crime was something that happened "over there," in the bad parts of town.

It wasn't a matter of rubber hoses or the "third degree," either. Lyons had no patience for those kind of strong-arm tactics. It would be too much like being a bully, using status as a cop to push people around.

No, the courts were talking about perfection. Hyper-technicalities. One time, evidence had been thrown out because a killer, who happened not to have reached his eighteenth birthday, wasn't advised by the police that he had a right to talk to his grandmother or other relatives, as well as to an attorney.

Judge Mayer loved those cases.

He loved them almost as much as he hated cops and prosecutors. Hell, almost as much as he resented Eva Connelly.

Eva was the busty young court reporter assigned to Judge Mayer's courtroom. Her crime had been to tell him she would rather be dead in a ditch than go to bed with him.

She'd regret that. Judge Mayer would see to that. By God, she'd regret it. But in the meantime he took out his frustrations by being even more high-handed than usual. That meant pretending that he didn't like the Supreme Court rules, but using them to throw out case after case.

Most of those cases would have been upheld had they happend to go before a different judge.

"I'm sorry, officer," he would say when making his ruling. "What you did sounds reasonable to *me*. If this criminal had been in *my* neighborhood, I'd want you to do the very same thing. But the Supreme Court doesn't see it that way. The law's the law, and I am bound to follow it, even if I don't like it. Case dismissed."

The cops and D.A.'s knew this was a crock of shit. So did the criminals. One crook even asked Judge Mayer if it meant he got to keep the TV sets he had stolen, after the judge ruled the police had detained him unreasonably.

"No, young man," said the judge firmly, "your constitutional rights don't go that far."

"Yet," muttered the Deputy D.A. disgustedly.

The young man's response had been equally succinct.

"Well, shee-it."

Of course, the California Supreme Court did make a good scapegoat. Cops and prosecutors alike found it convenient to blame the court when cases went bad. Sometimes the blame was appropriate; sometimes it was not.

"Rosie and The Reversals," as the Supreme Court was sometimes called—based on the name of their Chief Justice, Rose Bird, and the courts prodefendant rulings on so many cases—seemed to enjoy suppressing evidence or reversing convictions for almost any small procedural defect.

Still, it was especially galling when Judge Mayer did it, because he was such a staunch philosophical fellow traveler.

In short, nobody and no entity were immune from the judge's caprice. And today, when his back hurt and he had a hangover, the parties to the cases before him were in for a real treat.

As the clerk called the first case, Judge Mayer allowed his gaze to slide over, as it often did, to where Eva sat, stroking the keys of her steno machine. Resentment flared in him like a hot flame.

On a bad day Eva looked good. And this day was nowhere near a bad day.

Today, she looked stunning.

Thick, dark hair. Dark eyes. Somewhat on the tall side of average. Her chest was definitely on the large side of average. Substantially so. So much so that many observers didn't see much else.

She had on a crisp, severe white shirt, which was buttoned clear up to her neck. The button just below her breasts strained against its threads. The two sides of the shirt gapped, and Judge Mayer longed to gape at the view. She wore a black skirt, equally severe, which served only to emphasize the curve of her hips.

Through his lust, Judge Mayer despised her.

He had done so ever since that time she had turned him down.

He hated her for that.

The judge knew how handsome he was, with his dramatic mane of white hair above a tanned and relatively unlined face. He fancied the effect was a combination of university professor and country lawyer, dressed, however, in a seven-hundred-dollar suit.

"Daniel Webster goes to Harvard and meets *Gentleman's Quarterly*," one of the local prosecutors once remarked sourly.

Eva had declined his offer. At first she had been polite but firm. Later, however, she had invoked more firmness than politeness.

"No, Judge," she had insisted. Then she thought for a moment. "Wait a minute. Let me rephrase that. Not 'no,' but hell no!"

Still, Judge Mayer persisted. Still, Eva refused.

Finally he decided to approach it from a more businesslike angle. Sweeten the pot a little, so to speak. So he had hinted at how it couldn't hurt Eva's career if she slept with him. It might even advance it, he suggested. There were a lot of court reporters, after all, and assignments for reporting and transcribing certain of the lengthy—and therefore more lucrative—trials were chosen at random.

"Maybe I could whisper in Lady Luck's ear," he had proposed with a smile. "Especially if you whisper in mine."

Eva had been singularly unimpressed by the suggestion.

She had been so unimpressed, in fact, that she had responded in no uncertain terms and with a certain degree of heat that he was a despicable louse, that her goddamn career didn't need any help like that and that if he so much as thought about it again, she'd file a sexual harassment suit so fast that it would make his head spin.

After her boyfriend got through with him, that is.

The bit about the boyfriend troubled Judge Mayer, in a couple of ways.

He knew that Eva had been dating a deputy sheriff in the San Diego Sheriff's Department. Judge Mayer had seen the guy a couple of times when he'd stopped by to see Eva. His name was Johnny somebody or another, and apparently he taught defensive tactics at the Sheriff's Academy.

Goddamn neanderthal, the Judge thought. What's she see in a guy like that? Especially when she could be with me. And, he ruminated, get assigned to a big case. *After* she put out, of course.

Also troubling was the fact that Johnny lifted weights when he wasn't teaching judo or breaking up bar fights between members of outlaw motorcycle gangs.

Very definitely on the muscular side, the judge recalled. A little like that blond guy sitting in the back of the court. "Buffed out," to use a term he had heard one of the other court clerks whisper to a friend, in connection with some other ruggedly macho type.

Judge Mayer had no doubt about Johnny's ability to tie him into a pretzel. And even more troubling was the fact that it was just possible that Johnny might actually do it, if Eva told him about the judge's proposal.

Sometimes these cops had a certain wild streak to them. It was a crazy, primitive tendency, of course. Still, guys like that just might ignore the fact he was a judge if they learned he was using his position to put the moves on their girlfriends.

In Judge Mayer's eyes, Eva's boyfriend Johnny was just that type.

But Judge Mayer resented Eva—and Johnny—for another reason, as well, something that had nothing to do with fear. Instead, it had to do with something he had overheard called "glowing."

Like "buffed out," the term "glowing" was not a familiar term in Judge Mayer's vocabulary. He first learned about it when he happened to be listening in on a telephone conversation between a couple of the young clerks who worked in the courthouse.

Eavesdropping, actually.

Shortly after Eva had declined to sleep with him, Judge Mayer had happened to accidentally pick up the wrong line on the phone.

"Evie spent the weekend with Johnny," a woman's voice was saying in conspiratorial tones. Judge Mayer recognized the speaker as one of the other clerks and decided to listen in on the call.

"Oh, yeah?" whispered Clerk Two. She had heard the click when Judge Mayer picked up his own telephone, but she attributed it to the routine line noise in the cheap and outdated county phones. "I know she was going to, but I heard they had to cancel it. Like he had to work or something."

"They thought so, but then I guess he was able to get off after all."

Clerk Two giggled. "I bet he was able to 'get off,'" she said, in a not-so-veiled reference to the sexual interpretation of the phrase. "But was Eva?" A peal of earthy laughter followed her question.

"I didn't mean it that way," came the laughing protest. "But since you asked, the answer is, 'you better believe it.'" Clerk One's giggle was as conspiratorial as Clerk Two's had been.

A pause followed. "How do you know? Did you talk to her? Did she say that?"

"She didn't have to. She's just got that glow to her, you know? That look you only get from one thing, if you know what I mean."

"No kidding? Really?" Clerk Two's voice had a tone of hushed awe to it.

"Really."

There was a long pause, then Clerk Two giggled again. "I'd let Johnny make me glow any time."

"Yeah. Me, too. Evie'd not be too happy about it, though."

Later on that morning, Judge Mayer had made it a point to find Eva. Finally, he walked down to the offices where the court reporters worked, on the pretext of looking for the transcript on some hearing or another.

He had to admit "glowing" was a good term for how she looked.

She had that faraway look of relaxed satisfaction, a slight inward smile that bespoke sweet sensations and pleasant memories. Her movements were languid, and she seemed particularly given to making long, slow sighs of contentment.

In a completely irrational way, Judge Mayer despised both Eva and Johnny for that.

Today, as he looked down from the bench, he wondered what it would be like to make a woman look like that, to give her that glow.

Judge Mayer spent a lot of time looking around for the telltale glow. Usually he saw it on what he, Judge Donald Mayer, civil libertarian and egalitarian, liked to refer to as the "lower classes." The workers. Blue collar types. The men and women who get things done, while the Judge Mayers of the world make big, high-sounding talk.

He saw it on secretaries and clerks and typists, and their working-class husbands and boyfriends, the steelworkers, cops, and truck drivers, the heavy equipment operators, electrical linemen and construction workers. Rock singers. And members of the military—the army, navy, marine corps.

Goddamn them all, he thought. Men and women alike. Even if they did glow. The Eva Connellys and Johnny somebody or others of the world. All those lower types who didn't appreciate people like himself.

"Your Honor."

With a start, Judge Mayer realized they were on the fourth case already.

He couldn't even remember the first three. Probably they were so-called "stipulations," cases, in which the two attorneys had already agreed on what should happen and just needed the formality of his approval. Presumably he had given that.

Judge Mayer suppressed a groan. He recognized the speaker as John Adleigh, a bearded public defender. Before the lawyer could say anything more, the judge knew what was going to spew forth from his mouth. And he despised Adleigh, although he generally agreed with his arguments.

Adleigh began speaking.

His client was innocent. He only got convicted because of a miscarriage of justice.

And even if his client weren't innocent, it was a conspiracy. The prosecution and the police were engaged in a massive, vindictive plot, designed to single out this particular rapist for special oppression.

He was going to appeal the case to the Supreme Court if the judge didn't rule his way and throw it out of court.

And the present rapes, as well as any minor transgressions that his client might have done in the past, were due to a bad childhood and narcotics. It wasn't the defendant's fault, because drugs were a problem everywhere and the cops and courts simply weren't dealing with the problem. His parents hadn't raised him properly, and the school system had failed him.

Judge Mayer glanced at the other table to see who the D.A. was.

Oh, hell, he thought, not him.

He knew the guy from other cases. Hard-nosed and aggressive, this prosecutor was the sort of primitive who believed that victims of violent crime were entitled to receive a certain amount of visceral satisfaction—vengeance, to put it bluntly—from the court's sentence. This D.A. didn't believe that being under the influence of drugs was an excuse for raping or killing people, at least where nobody held a gun to the crook's head and made the crook take the drugs.

Arguments like that held a sort of superficial appeal, especially to the unenlightened public.

The Eva Connellys and the Johnny whoevers of the world would probably believe such theories. And this D.A.—why did he have to be assigned to Judge Mayer's courtroom today? It wasn't going to be easy to hand out lenient sentences with him in attendance.

With a sigh Judge Mayer bent to his task.

CARL LYONS LISTENED disgustedly to the proceedings.

Things hadn't changed a bit since he was a cop, he thought. If anything, they've gotten worse, in California, at least.

He hadn't kept up on the law since he left the select state/federal strike force for which he'd been recruited from the Los Angeles Police Department. Vague rumors existed that at least the U.S. Supreme Court was backing away from the extreme procriminal position of the Warren court in the sixties and seventies. But that didn't affect California, and the blond man didn't like what he was hearing.

As the defense attorney continued his palaver of all the factors except free will, choice and evil intent that had caused his client to commit the rapes, Lyons suppressed a sigh.

Hell, he thought, the whole platoon's out of step except this one guy. To hear the attorney, we ought to be giving this guy a medal, not sending him to prison. After all, he's a young man, only a lad.

And this crap that the defense attorney was dishing out so liberally—didn't he know that hardly anybody listened to it?

Suddenly, irrationally, Lyons felt better. The system wasn't great, but it wasn't all bad. What the hell, it was one hell of a lot better than some systems, where the government could tell you what "patter" you could say and what you couldn't.

Types like Judge Mayer existed everywhere, of course. But so did others—the good judges, guys like the D.A., up there, pumping away against the bilge spewed forth by the defense attorney. People like most of the cops and witnesses in this very courtroom, good people, who worked a day for a day's pay.

And once in a while, when the system failed, or faltered, other good men came forward.

Usually the public never saw them.

They were loners, for the most part, though they worked as a team.

Men like Rosario "the Politician" Blancanales, former Green Beret, with dark good looks and a smile that could charm a tax collector. Airborne, jungle warfare school, and master of innumerable ways to kill.

Men like Hermann "Gadgets" Schwarz, the genius with metaphysical tendencies in mind control, master at electronics, survivor of severe and enthusiastic infliction of physical pain at the hands of the Mafia. When they asked him how he managed that, he shrugged and said he didn't recall it, he was out walking his dog.

These were the men of Stony Man Farm's Able Team.

The judge finished giving the young rapist a light sentence and a stern lecture. The defendant, who had already been given enough last chances by different judges over the years and knew that a show of contrition was helpful in such cases, said, "Yes, sir, Your Honor." Then the clerk called for a recess, and the shuffling of feet was repeated.

As Lyons got to his feet he caught the gaze of a couple of plainclothes detectives with the San Diego Sheriff's Department, also making their way out of the courtroom.

"You a cop?" one of them asked.

Lyons nodded. He'd set the record straight later, by explaining that he was attached to a federal strike force. He wasn't, not officially, at least, but it was close enough. After all, most of his missions came from the government, at least indirectly.

He recognized that the cop's question meant that he, Lyons, still must have "that look" about him, the indefinable something that enables the good guys everywhere to recognize another of their own.

The deputy sheriff was speaking again. "We're going to get some coffee here. Want to join us?"

"Think there's time?"

"Are you kidding? With this judge, we could go have breakfast. Come on. Let's go."

Lyons nodded. "Right on." Some things don't change, he thought.

As they went out of the courtroom he wondered idly how it was that Judge Mayer had come to the interest of Hal Brognola. And, more to the point, if he, Carl Lyons, would have the pleasure of being involved.

Somehow, he hoped so.

5

Carl Lyons walked with the two detectives down the long hallway toward the elevators. They would have to take the elevator down to the coffee shop.

At that moment his only conscious thought was that it would be good to pass the time by chatting with the two men. Also, it would be even better to get away from the mindless patter of Judge Mayer's courtroom.

A psychiatrist might have given another explanation.

Subconsciously, perhaps, it also represented a small chance to revisit the past. Those had been days when he had enjoyed the camaraderie of the police department, back when he had been an idealistic young cop. But now that was ancient history, before Stony Man Farm had turned him into something of a lone wolf.

An occupational hazard, the shrink would say. And Lyons would agree. The job demanded it.

"He travels the fastest who travels alone."

What neither Lyons nor the imaginary shrink could have known was that the seemingly innocent invitation would be the first step into a battlefield as bloody as any he had ever encountered.

The coffee shop on the fourth floor of the county courthouse wasn't a real live coffee shop, Lyons realized when he got there. He saw nothing but a bunch of vending machines adjacent to eight or ten cheap Formica tables and even cheaper plastic chairs.

Oval-shaped brown stains spotted the linoleum floor where cigarettes had been crushed out. The coffee shop provided what were supposed to be ashtrays in the form of cheap tin disks with corrugated edges. Lyons idly picked one up and examined it.

Lyons dropped the piece of tin to the floor and crushed it under his heel. Afterward he felt a pang of regret—it had been a stupid and childish stunt, and not much of an example, either.

"Black?"

The voice came from the stocky, dark-complected officer, the one who had issued the invitation for Lyons to join them.

Lyons nodded and started to fish into his pocket for some change. The cop shook his head. "On me."

"Thanks," responded the Ironman simply. Then, extending his hand, he introduced himself. "Carl Lyons."

"I'm Vince Ceri," the detective buying the coffee said. "This dirt bag—" he nodded good-naturedly toward the tall, young-looking man with sandy red hair "—is Pat Adams."

They collared one of the tables and sat down. The table rocked from side to side, unstable because the single steel pedestal on which it rested was missing the "foot" on one side of its base.

Ceri shook his head disgustedly, then took a green sheet of paper from inside his coat pocket. He unfolded it and glanced at it, then nodded and tore it in half. Ceri folded one half over and over, making a small, thick square of green paper. He bent forward and wedged the square under the side of the pedestal's base that was missing the foot. He tried to shake the table, then gave a grunt of satisfaction.

Sitting up again, he crumpled the other half of the sheet into a wadded ball. Glancing around the room, he found the plastic wastebasket in one corner. With a wink, he hooked the paper ball skillfully into the container and turned back to his coffee.

"Subpoena," he said simply, in response to Lyons's unspoken question.

Lyons grinned. "Good use for it."

As conversation developed, Lyons learned that Vinnie and Pat were detectives with the San Diego Sheriff's Department, both assigned to the Major Crimes Division. For his part, Lyons said he had been with the L.A.P.D. and was now attached to a Federal Justice Department Strike Force.

"You wouldn't by any chance be involved in that National City caper, would you?" asked Vinnie casually.

"What's that?" responded Lyons.

"That stiff they found down in National City last week."

"I didn't hear about it."

Vinnie rolled his eyes at his partner. "Yeah, yeah, yeah," he said in good-natured disgust. "You get that, Pat? He didn't hear about it."

Adams shook his head. "Coincidence. Gotta be. Sheer, unbelievable, one in a million coincidence. Big-shot federal-strike-force guy just happens to show up in court after some CI gets iced, checking out the same judge that the dead guy had been in front of.''

"Coincidence," agreed Vinnie. "I don't hear him saying anything else."

"Me, either. Fact is, I don't hear him saying anything. And after you bought him coffee, no less." Adams made a clucking sound with his tongue. "Helluva note. Must be something they teach in Fed school."

Lyons grinned sheepishly.

He knew what they were talking about. Hell, he'd run into the same thing himself, years back, when he was a street cop. All federal officers were notoriously closemouthed, and, generally, were condescendingly so.

Occasionally, of course, it happened that the federal agent was *not* holding back. Like now. He didn't have any idea about the stiff down in National City, as Vinnie Ceri had called it. That wasn't why he was there at all.

Or was it?

The question nagged at Lyons's subconscious. He shoved it aside. Time enough to deal with that later. For now, all he could do was grin and bear it, put up with their kidding skepticism. Good-natured as it all was, Vinnie and Adams would come around to believing him. Probably.

Sharing with the Feds is a one-way street, the locals used to say.

Pooling information meant tell us everything you know, and then we'll tell you if we can discuss it. There was a story about a local cop who once provided some useful intelligence to the FBI as part of a cooperative venture. A week later—when he wanted to refresh his memory about what the informant had said—he was denied access to the very report he'd furnished in the first place.

Lyons figured the best way to handle Vinnie's and Adams' skepticism was not to protest too much.

He pitched his voice low and made it sound deliberately pompous.

"Hey, buddy, I'm a federal agent. Federal Five-O. My time is valuable, and it's so secret, if I told you, I'd have to kill you." Then he grinned. "Hell, it's so secret, they don't even tell *me* what I'm doing half the time."

It worked. Vinnie and Pat relaxed, and Vinnie grinned. "Hey, Lyons, you're okay. For a Fed, anyway."

"That's only 'cause he used to be a local," Adams observed. "Even if it was only PD, instead of SO," he added with a wink, referring to the rivalry that existed between city police departments and county sheriff's departments.

Lyons knew what Pat was talking about.

The rivalry was particularly acute in some of the big counties in California, including San Diego and, of course, Los Angeles, where he had been a cop.

In those places, urban sprawl meant that the cities had long since outgrown the city limits. The population would be as dense in the county as inside the city itself. There, the SO's—sheriff's offices—were apt to number five hundred or a thousand sworn officers, or more, bigger than all but the largest police departments.

Rivalry was inevitable. And, depending on the personalities involved, it was either friendly or, in some cases, somewhat less than that.

"So tell me about the National City caper," Lyons urged.

Vinnie looked closely at him. "You really don't know about it, then?"

Lyons shook his head. Vinnie shrugged and continued.

"A National City patrol officer stumbled onto a bunch of Cubans putting the old torture number to some guy in a warehouse down by the waterfront." His voice was deliberately casual and reflected the callousness that cops learn as a defense mechanism against the demands of the job.

"What happened?"

"These guys had some pitiful bastard clamped in a vise. Put his head in it and tightened it down a little, so he couldn't go anywhere while they worked on him. Then, when they got done with their fun and games, they kept tightening it down."

"It sort of made the guy narrow-minded, you might say," cracked Adams ghoulishly. "Molded his outlook, so to speak."

Lyons grimaced. He recalled how reputed Chicago mobster Tony "the Ant" Spilotro had been accused—and later acquitted—of something similar, the head-in-the-vise routine. Lyons had seen the pictures, and it hadn't been pretty.

"So, what happened when the National City officer intervened?" persisted Lyons.

"Well, there were at least four Cubans," said Vinnie. "The copper got two of 'em with a shotgun; the rest got away."

"Anybody talking?" inquired Lyons. "Any idea why they were doing this?"

"Are you kidding?" interjected Adams. "Officer had double-ought buck in the shotgun. Shot the shit out of the guys he hit. Killed 'em both."

"And the guy in the vise?"

"Dead. Hell of a way to go, too. Pathologist says he didn't die until they tightened it down, from what I hear."

Adams was watching Lyons closely. "You sure you're not doing something on it? You playing it straight with us?"

Lyons nodded. However, he wondered if he was, in fact, "doing something on it," without exactly knowing it.

He added up the facts in his mind.

Brognola calls him up, real casual like, and suggests he might want to drift down to San Diego to take care of a couple of minor items of business. Oh, yes, Ironman, and while you're down there, check out Judge Mayer.

And no, Lyons, you don't need to know *why* you're checking out Judge Mayer.

And now a body in a warehouse, tortured to death? And Vinnie letting it slip that the guy had just happened to have been up in court before Judge Mayer recently.

Coincidences do happen, of course. The guy on the front line was sometimes the last to know what was going on. Sometimes, hell. Almost always would be more like it.

And, in a perverse sort of way, Lyons didn't mind that. He almost liked it, in fact. Every operation could only have one boss. It only mattered that you trusted yours. Then it went with the territory that the man at the top should say "what" without saying "why.'

Lyons trusted his man at the top, Hal Brognola, chief of operations at Stony Man Farm, implicitly. With his life, to be exact.

"Any ideas why they did it?" he reiterated to Vinnie and Adams.

Ceri shrugged. "Hard to tell. My guess is that a big narcotics caper's involved somehow. "Snitch killing, maybe."

"Was the guy a CI for the narcs?" Lyons asked, using the acronym for "confidential informant," somebody who is providing intelligence information to a law enforcement agency.

"That's what we wondered if you knew about." said Vinnie with a faint smile. "I thought maybe he was working for some big federal operation."

It was Lyons's turn to shrug. "He may be, but nothing I know about. Of course there are so many agencies in the action, that doesn't mean much."

Vinnie cocked his head to one side. "From what I hear, it sounds like he might have been a snitch, all right."

"How so?"

"Just had that smell, you know? Hell, the torture routine, that could be anybody, but it has that foul odor of organized crime or narcotics."

"Those boys play rough," interjected Adams needlessly, but of course he didn't know Lyons's extensive background in the area.

Lyons nodded. Vinnie went on.

"And it was Cubans who did it. That sounds like big dope to me."

"How so?"

"Hell, San Diego is becoming Miami West these days. As the Feds put pressure on the East Coast, they're driving the big importers west. And a lot of the same guys who are well established in Miami are setting up shop, opening up routes, out here."

"Which explains the Cubans," mused Lyons.

"Yeah."

Lyons thought it over. "Sounds possible, I guess."

Vinnie Ceri took another sip of his coffee. "There's more." He paused and looked at the oily liquid in the bottom of the paper cup. Making a face, he set it aside and continued. He kept his voice low in the conspiratorial manner of cops sharing intelligence. He did it from force of habit—like the Feds, local cops were security conscious themselves—even though what he was about to say had been carried in all the papers.

"I hear the guy didn't have any criminal history. No background at all."

"I thought you said he had just been in front of this judge, Judge Dick-head or whatever it is," observed Lyons.

Vinnie nodded. "Yeah. That's true. On a possession caper. He got probation. But before that, nothing. Zip code. Nobody home. Absolutely no criminal record, no arrests, no convictions, nothing. It was like he was born yesterday or six months ago, anyway, right before he got the possession rap."

Lyons recalled Brognola's rebuke about not having a "need to know" about why he was checking up on Mayer. Well, to hell with him—to hell with Hal, he interrupted his own thoughts—even if he is the chief. If mission control wasn't going to fill in the gaps, it was only natural that the agents would do it themselves. That's what being a government operative was all about.

Now Lyons regarded it as a challenge to find out if his assignment to see Judge Mayer was, in fact, connected with the National City caper.

The sheriff's man interrupted his thoughts. "What's that sound like to you?"

"Sounds like witness protection," Lyons said slowly. "They could do that."

Vinnie leaned back in his chair and looked at his watch. "It sure does," he agreed. "They sure could," he added.

Lyons thought it over. The more he considered it, the more likely it sounded.

Confidential informants were often used in organized crime investigations. They were usually a monumental headache of course, but that was to be expected. Most informants were crooks themselves, who were only cooperating because they'd been caught by the cops. For them it was help out or go to jail. A lot of them got paid for their information of course, but that didn't make them any more reliable.

Still, CI's were a necessary evil. It simply wasn't possible to infiltrate the sophisticated organized criminal enterprises without them.

And of course they were crooks themselves. Who else but a crook would be sufficiently involved in the conspiracies to be of any assistance to law enforcement? And if it meant letting a few little fish go and even giving them money, so be it. It was worth it to get a shot at the bigger fish.

The bit about the complete absence of any criminal record on the man in the vise was a tantalizing bit of information, and one that fit with Vinnie's "big narcotics" theory.

Often, as part of the benefits of assisting in the investigation, the agents would give the CI a new identity. This had the effect of wiping the slate clean as far as his prior criminal record was concerned.

"Like he was born yesterday or six months ago, anyway," as Vinnie had put it.

Vinnie was checking his watch again. "Gotta get back into court," he announced. "Take it easy, Lyons. Good to meet you."

They shook hands all the way around. As they got into the elevator, Vinnie spoke again, "And if you change your mind about whether you were involved in this caper or not, Mr. Fed, and you ever want to let a buddy know what it was really all about, give me a call."

His voice was friendly, not as sarcastic as the words had been.

Lyons nodded. He had the sneaking suspicion that Vinnie was probably right after all. The Ironman's best guess now was that the Stony Man operation was in fact involved and just hadn't gotten around to telling their man in the field yet.

The more he thought about it, the more likely it sounded.

"You got it, Vinnie," he said, grinning. "And thanks."

The elevator door opened on the third floor, where Judge Mayer's courtroom was located, and the two sheriff's men got out. Lyons stayed inside.

As the doors closed he checked his watch. Just after ten, he noted.

What the hell. He wasn't doing anything else—why not drop down to the National City Police Department and see if he could talk to the homicide guys a little.

Nothing else to do, anyway.

6

The National City homicide detective's name was Tom Grogan. Shortly before noon Lyons presented himself at the counter of the PD, identified himself and asked for Grogan.

The bored desk officer looked him over carefully. "This about the warehouse caper?"

Lyons nodded.

"Have a seat. I'll see if I can locate him."

Five minutes later the door adjacent to the counter opened and Grogan emerged. The detective introduced himself, and they shook hands. Grogan escorted Lyons back into the detective division.

Lyons found himself wondering if Adams, one of the two sheriff's detectives he had been talking to, and Grogan were related in some way.

Like Adams, Grogan was tall and had reddish blond hair. Most of all, however, he showed the same dark sense of humor. He cracked the same kind of morbid jokes as Adams had, jiving about the unknown man's ghastly death. If anything, his wisecracks proved to be more blunt and less subtle than the sheriff's man's had been.

"One thing, Lyons, it made it easy when the pathologist wanted the guy's head for some kind of specialized tests he wanted to run."

Lyons sensed he was being set up. Keeping his face bland, he responded, "Oh, yeah? How's that?"

"Well, it was a lot easier to transport. Normally we have to use these big metal cases, like so." Grogan indicated with his hands a cube some ten to twelve inches on a side. "Didn't have to use that in this case, though."

Lyons played along. "Oh, yeah? What'd you use?"

"For this guy, we just used a shoe box. Fit real well, you know? Long and skinny?"

Lyons forced an obligatory grin.

"Must've surprised the guy, though," Grogan continued. "What they did to him, I mean."

"Why's that?"

"His eyes were bugging out."

Lyons groaned to acknowledge the wisecrack.

"Embarrassed the guy, though," Grogan continued.

"Oh, yeah?"

"Yeah. Made his face red."

The Ironman sensed this could go on all day unless he did something about it. Still, he had no official authority to find out what was going on in the case, and the National City man was certainly not obligated to tell him. And for all Grogan's friendly humor, Lyons could tell the guy was a pro. Consistent with that, he wasn't going to open his case file to just anybody— including another cop or somebody from some federal strike force—who walked in off the street.

In fact, Lyons got the distinct impression that he was being sized up by the detective, that the grim patter was just cover while Grogan evaluated things.

Lyons knew Grogan wouldn't take him at face value. Because of this he had gone by his motel and picked up the badge and credentials that he always carried concealed in the lining of his suitcase. That way, when he presented himself at the counter of the NCPD, he at least had something to show he was legit. "Emblems of authority," he had once heard it called.

The official ID's had been the brainchild, appropriately enough, of Stony Man's chief brain, Aaron "the Bear" Kurtzman.

Rumpled and hairy, Kurtzman resembled Smoky the Bear with a hangover. As the informal intelligence officer of the Stony Man Operation, the Bear had assembled a computer setup that was rivaled only by the NSA, the National Security Agency. To be sure, in terms of sheer numbers, the NSA had more computers. But in terms of the sophistication of the systems, the Bear's own hardware was second to none.

The Bear had pushed for the ID's. This meant that he had to first sell Brognola on the idea.

His reasoning made sense, particularly for Able Team. Lyons and the others, it seemed, had by a process of evolution ended up focusing their efforts chiefly on domestic urban terrorism. Though they occasionally got plugged into overseas operations, most of their work was done inside the U.S.

"That means you have to interface with the locals," as the Bear had explained it.

Lyons had wrinkled his brow. "Do what?" he inquired.

It was Gadgets Schwarz, himself an electronics and computer whiz, who had given the reply. "Interface, pal."

"What's that?"

"This is the computer age, man," said Gadgets with a wink. "That's microchip talk for hook up with. Work together. Interact with. Join forces."

"Oh."

"Get with the program, Ironman."

In the pause that followed, Blancanales allowed just a hint of his politician's smile to trace his lips. "I've interfaced with a few locals before."

Gadgets played straight man. "I'm sure you have. How was it, anyway?"

"Very pleasant, thank you. Altogether, rather enjoyable experiences, if you know what I mean."

"I wonder if the ladies would say the same thing," muttered Lyons.

Blancanales pretended to look wounded, then affectedly breathed on his fingernails and polished them on his lapel. "I'm quite confident they would," he said modestly.

"How do you feel about continuing those activities, doing some further interfacing, so to speak?" persisted Gadgets.

"Quite good, actually." Blancanales groped in his own mind for some appropriate computer term he could throw back. Then he came up with one. "Provided the other party is 'user friendly,' of course."

"Menu-operated?" suggested Gadgets quickly, never at a loss for computer or programming terms. "Hard-disk drive?"

"That's better than a floppy one," rejoined the Politician. "If you know what I mean."

Lyons had regarded his two partners with good-natured disgust. "All right, all right," he said finally. "So I'm..."

Sensing Lyons was trying to call a halt to the kidding, Gadgets interrupted him quickly. "One more," he said with a wink. "Did you use your Wang?" he asked Blancanales, referring to a popular computer brand, if not to something else.

"As a matter of fact..."

It was Lyons's turn to interrupt. "So I'm not up on the high tech end of things," he finished.

"Obviously," kidded Gadgets. "Still back in the age of IBM cards, Ironman? Do not fold, spindle or mutilate?"

"Yeah," Blancanales remarked with elaborate casualness, affecting to speak to nobody in particular.

"Lyons is from the old school. Kick ass and take names. They didn't have computers back when he was a cop. He's done his share of interfacing, himself, though."

"How so?" asked Gadgets.

"He used to date a lady cop, I hear. Problem was, whenever he said, 'assume the position,' she never knew if he wanted to conduct a pat-down search for weapons or make love."

Lyons made a fake grimace of anger. Before he could respond, however, the Bear intervened.

"About the badges," he began. "They could prove to be helpful whenever you have to, uh—" he groped for a word other than interface "—work with other groups or agencies, either local officers or the Feds.

Especially since most of your work is done State-side."

Gadgets nodded. "Makes sense, actually. Might help open a few doors, at that."

Strangely, it was Lyons, the former cop, who had resisted the idea at first.

"We're not cops," he argued. "Cops enforce the laws. We don't. We take up where they can't, no reflection on them, of course." Then he added, "Besides, most cops and Feds I've worked with take a dim view of people waving around fake ID's. It's a crime, in fact."

Kurtzman looked at him, his jaw tight.

"These aren't going to be fake at all. They'll show that you're specially commissioned operatives for a special branch of the State Department, or Justice Department, maybe. Which you will be. Sort of, anyway. So what's the problem with having them?"

"I still don't like it."

"So, tell me why not?"

"Look," said Lyons. "A badge helps a cop—usually, that is, unless somebody wants to stick it up your ass—because it is a symbol of authority. It tells people you've got the power of the law behind you, such as it is."

"So?"

"So we're not like that. We operate in secret. More like spies or commandos than cops. Hell, most of the time, the government—and the law—will have to disown us, if we fuck up. And I, for one, don't relish falling into the hands of the bad guys when I'm undercover, only to have them find out I'm working for some government organization."

"Nobody's asking you to carry it, for God's sake," retorted the Bear, a little irritated. "Just have it available, in case some other agency you have to work with wants proof of who you are."

Reluctantly Lyons had agreed. That had been some six months ago. Now, as he faced Detective Grogan in the National City Police Department, the Ironman realized that, as usual, the Bear had been right on the money.

Grogan had evidently finished foxing around and decided that the straightforward approach was the best one.

"So," he said at last, "what's your interest in the Excedrin caper?"

"Excedrin caper?"

"Just imagine the headache that guy must have had."

Lyons let it pass. In response he decided to use the famed federal secrecy to his advantage, if he could. Stretching the truth a little, he responded, "I'm supposed to check the guy out a little, see if it ties in with a caper we've got going."

"Was the guy an informant of yours?"

"That's possible. I can't tell until I find out a little more about it."

"Hell," said Grogan, "that should be my line."

"How so?"

"We don't even have a good ID on the guy yet. We know that he got arrested here for a minor possession beef. Got put on probation down here maybe three, four months ago. But before that, zippo."

"FBI raps show anything?" asked Lyons casually.

"Totally clean. Nothing. And, believe me, this guy wasn't clean. I've been around enough to be able to tell. And this guy had been around the block. In fact`...`"

He paused. Lyons didn't interrupt.

"In fact, he had the look of somebody who had 'been around' quite a bit, then went clean for a while. And now he was backsliding. It's nothing definite; that's just a feel I get about the guy."

"Sounds like he could be a snitch," Lyons said to show Grogan he had some background in the area and to open the door for some mutual cooperation. Grogan accepted the invitation.

"What can you do for me, if I let you in on it?"

Lyons shrugged. "Don't know. Maybe nothing. Maybe something. If I can, I will, though."

Grogan evaluated that. "Okay. But no copies of any reports unless you go through the chief."

"That's fair enough."

Lyons sat down in the chair Grogan waved him into. Grogan reached for a thick file of stiff, dark red cardboard. Next to the file was a bakery box of donuts and sweet rolls. He shoved the box to Lyons.

"Have one," he grunted absentmindedly as he began to open the file. "Lunch," he added. "It's the only lunch I'll get today," he mourned good-naturedly.

Normally the Ironman didn't eat much food of that type.

It wasn't that he was a light eater—he was well-known around Stony Man for the amount of food he would and usually did eat. But usually, it was steak and eggs, heavy on protein and heavy on carbohydrates other than those that came with sweet rolls. Once when asked about his cholesterol intake, he had responded that only a damn fool or a complete optimist would worry that any member of Able Team might die of hardening of the arteries.

"As if we should live that long," he had said with a wink.

Today, though, he sensed he was being tested.

Something about the elaborately casual manner in which Grogan had pushed the rolls over to him at that particular moment led him to believe that photographs would be next. And if that were so, he could bet the pics would be gruesome.

Lyons could also sense that at that moment he and Grogan were the center of attention of the other detectives in the room. In a subtle way the men had stopped whatever they had been working on and were watching his reaction.

Of course there was nothing wrong with that. In another time and place, as a young cop bursting with muscles and machismo, Lyons had done similar things.

Still, he'd be damned if he'd let Grogan get to him. It was a point of professional pride, in a sense.

"Thanks," he said simply, reaching for the box of pastries.

He scanned them and saw immediately which one he would take. It was some kind of sweet roll, long and filled with raspberry jam. A scattering of sliced nuts, almonds probably, covered the jam, and the whole mess was topped with a white melted sugar frosting.

Though he tried to conceal it, Grogan looked pleased when Lyons made that selection. This only confirmed the Ironman's suspicion that he was being set up.

Off to one side, Lyons caught—but ignored—the wink one of the other investigators shot to his buddy.

He took a bite of the pastry just as Grogan slid a stack of four-by-five-inch photographs out of the folder.

It was gruesome, all right. Clear, focused pictures of the homicide scene. In living color.

Or dead color, to be more accurate.

The gory countenance of the dead man, his head squeezed between the jaws of the heavy vise, stared up at Lyons.

Lyons chewed thoughtfully while he studied the picture. Then, using his left index finger, he slid the picture even closer and squared it around so he was looking straight at it.

And took another bite.

Grogan's disappointment was evident. The other cops grinned at each other. Now, however, it was Grogan who was the object of their amusement.

From the corner of his eye Lyons saw some of the raspberry start to drip from the roll.

Time for the coup de grace, the grand slam.

Casually he pretended to concentrate on the photo, ignoring the sweet roll. Then his hand just happened to let the glob of raspberry fall off.

It fell directly on the glossy picture, squarely on the pool of blood that surrounded one of the dead Cubans.

"Oh, shit," he muttered distractedly.

Using his left index finger, he mopped up the jam from the slick surface of the photograph. Almost absentmindedly he licked the sweet from his finger.

"Sorry about that, Tom," he said to Grogan, then resumed his study of the other pics.

Unable to be surreptitious any longer, one of the other detectives smacked his hand down on the table and laughed out loud.

"Damn good pastry," Lyons said to Grogan. "Hey, you notice how the nuts and the frosting sort of look like this guy's skull and brains in the picture here? Kinda the same color, anyway." He took another bite. Then, he, too, couldn't contain himself any longer and broke into open laughter.

Grogan grinned sheepishly. "Okay, okay," he said. "So I was trying to gross you out. I confess it. But you kicked my ass on that one."

The tension was broken. Lyons's authenticity had been established, even if he were a Fed, as one of the men remarked later. Grogan opened the file and started sorting through it, typewritten reports, hand-printed reports, lab reports, the autopsy report, all the carefully assembled paper on the Excedrin man.

As for Lyons, he kept munching the sweet roll until it was all gone. He licked his fingers and wiped them on a tissue. Then he used the same tissue, only a different part of it, to wipe the last traces of jam from the photograph.

As he did so, his mind thought two separate but related things.

First, his casual gag with the sweet roll had been one of the hardest things he had ever done.

It wasn't because of the gore in the photograph—hell, he'd seen enough death to be well beyond that. No, it had been much more personal than that, ten times as much of a kick in the guts.

He knew the guy in the photo.

Of all the things he could have expected, that had been the farthest from his mind.

What had been so difficult was keeping his expression bland, wearing the poker face. He thought he'd pulled it off. He hoped so. None of the detectives seemed to notice, anyway, and any funny look he may have exhibited would probably be attributed to the stunt with the jam.

In any event, he couldn't let Grogan know that he recognized the body.

He hated to hold out on the National City detective. It was just the kind of thing that they complained about. But he had no choice, until he had talked to Brognola and found out what was going on.

He glanced at the picture again.

Danny Forbes. Unmistakably Danny Forbes, despite the distortion to his face from the skull-popping pressure of the vise.

Lyons had arrested him, recruited him, made cases with him, sent men to prison because of him.

He also knew that Danny had come to idolize him.

It wasn't vanity. Maybe it wasn't even that much of a compliment, Danny being what he was. But the simple fact remained that Lyons was probably the first human being who had ever been completely fair and square with Danny Forbes.

When Danny fucked up, Lyons knew about it, of course. And if it was on purpose, the Ironman was quick to, in the strike force jargon, "take corrective actions." That sometimes meant taking Danny and kicking his skinny informant's ass. But when it was a simple human error, Lyons let it slide—hell, he wouldn't have thought of doing anything else.

And when Danny did a good job, literally laying his life on the line to make a drug buy for the agents, Lyons recognized that also and praised him.

That was what had surprised Danny the most, that Lyons judged his acts—what he *did*—good or bad, without criticizing what he *was*.

"You're straight up, Mr. Lyons," Danny had once said.

And now Danny was the Excedrin man.

That led to the second thing that had been on Lyons's mind when he saw the photo and realized who it was. Actually, it was a mixture of things.

First he felt pity, but it became more personal than that. He felt anger, then sorrow and maybe a little guilt.

The sorrow part had surprised him a little. But now as he analyzed his feelings, they made sense. Part of it was based on the simple fact that Lyons had known Danny; the death of somebody you know always makes a bigger impact than somebody you don't, he realized. A child starves to death in Ethiopia, and the puppy that belongs to your neighbor's kid gets hit by a car, Lyons thought—which one puts a lump in your throat?

But it was more than just knowing Danny Forbes. Besides that, Lyons had liked him. And somebody, these Cubans, had treated him very badly.

The Ironman didn't like that.

Lyons glanced at the deformed face, crushed between the jaws of the vise. Already his mind was at work combining instinct, experience and smarts as he analyzed what little he knew.

Cubans.

That meant Florida, almost surely. Miami, probably.

The murder also fit with big narcotics, as the two sheriff's detectives, Vinnie and Pat, had guessed. And dope had been Danny's area of operation as an informant. He hadn't been an insider in some organized crime extortion or gambling ring.

So Danny had made somebody angry. Probably that had happened because he made a case against whoever it was.

That "somebody" had sicced the dogs on Danny. Cuban dogs, vicious bastards who enjoyed their work.

Their work would include killing Danny, of course. It would include making him die hard, to punish him and to get the word out on the streets that if you fuck with "somebody" this is what happens. But, Lyons knew, it was more than just punishment and a message.

They would have interrogated Danny before they killed him.

Whom had he told on? What other cases was he being used on? Was there something else in the mill, some other indictment waiting to be unsealed? How much did the Feds know? Who were their big targets?

Even Lyons couldn't bring himself to try to imagine how Danny Forbes had spent his last hours in this world.

So the Cuban dogs had gone after Danny. And they'd caught up with him. Maybe they had made wisecracks as they tortured Danny to death, joking about putting the squeeze to him, perhaps. But as Lyons scanned the reports in Grogan's file and looked at the photographs, he began to get a feel for something else about the Cubans, especially the leader.

It crystallized in his mind as he read the report by McMurray, the National City cop who had broken up the party. The report described the way the men had scattered and how the leader had sort of vanished ninjalike when McMurray started shooting.

Sure they were pros, especially the leader. But more than that, Lyons began to get the feel that the Cubans had enjoyed what they were doing.

That made them twice as dangerous.

Almost as dangerous as Lyons himself.

7

Even before Lyons opened the door to his motel room, he knew that somebody had been inside while he was gone.

Knowing that was no big deal, actually. It was elementary trade-craft, something he learned to do, something he had practiced until it became automatic.

The training had begun even back when he was a street cop. Some of it was simple, basic stuff, he knew, but it could save your life. Never stand in front of a door when you knock on it, stand off to one side in case whoever was inside started shooting through the door. Always position yourself to keep your sidearm away from whomever you are talking to—why make it easy for them to get your gun?

Practice until it becomes automatic.

It had never ceased to amaze him how many cops never bothered to learn even these and other rudimentary officer survival techniques. But a lot of them don't, and every year across the country a shockingly high number of them died.

The learning process continued.

When he was a member of the elite Federal Organized Crime Strike Force, for which he had been recruited while still on the LAPD, the tools had become more sophisticated. After a few months on the strike force, during which Lyons's rugged abilities and unshakeable integrity had been established, the Justice Department had arranged for him to receive some special training.

It had not been something most federal agents are exposed to.

Most members of the FBI go their whole careers without even knowing these schools exist. Ditto, the U.S. Marshals, the Secret Service, the CIA and the NSA. But from each agency a handful of carefully selected men and women will be chosen to master the weaponry and survival skills necessary to function on the cutting edge of national security operations.

These weren't the desk officers. These were the field men, the executives—in the sense of "executing" or carrying out a plan—that nether group of shadow operatives who were doing it, not directing it.

Lyons, as a street cop turned organized crime investigator, had no need for jungle survival skills. His training had focused on urban combat techniques, fighting and running in the streets, the alleys, the darkened hallways of tenements, and in the chrome and glass of modern skyscrapers.

Early on, too, he had learned ways to tell if somebody had invaded his cave while he was out.

A hair placed "just so" on the doorknob or the lock, or on one of the hinges, perhaps. Or place one of those little round circles of paper that is left after a hole is punched in a sheet of paper on the upper surface of the door, below the jamb, or at a certain location.

These things had become as automatic as zipping his fly when he put on his pants.

Today, as he returned to the motel room after his meeting with Detective Grogan, Lyons saw immediately that his little signs had all been disturbed.

Instantly he was on full alert.

So, he thought, something was up, after all. The opening gambits were beginning. Whoever was inside the room, whether foe or friend—it at least meant that things were moving.

His mind raced through the possibilities as he scanned the several little traps he had put out before leaving. Always use more than one, he had been taught. Make one or two obvious, because somebody might be trying to be really cute, by looking for the signs so they can be put back. In that case, the intruder may replace only a couple and think he's gotten them all.

Here, though, even the obvious ones were not in place.

He glanced around the floor. No sign of them. Nothing. Zero. Zip.

If it had been somebody like a maid who had entered—even though he had specifically called the desk and requested no maid service when he left—the signs should be scattered about the floor where they would have fallen.

But they weren't in place, and they weren't lying anywhere in sight. That could only mean one thing.

Whoever had entered knew enough to look for his little markers. He, or she, knew they would be there. That meant the intruder knew Lyons or at least knew

about his modus operandi. Moreover, having found
the signs, whoever it was had also collected them.

The message was clear. Hell, it might as well have
been written on a note taped to the wall.

"I've been inside," the message was telling him. "I
came to your room and I found your little telltale
signs. I went inside, and I don't give a damn if you
know or not. In fact, I took 'em to tell you I was
here."

That meant a couple of possibilities.

It was a friend. Or if not a friend, then a foe who
had come and gone, who wasn't inside now. Hell, if it
was an enemy who knew enough about him to look for
his signs, the guy would be a pro. And a pro wouldn't
plan to wait inside, ready to ambush him, after being
so obvious about his entry.

Unless the guy was real tricky and could guess this
would be Lyons's reaction....

His mind sifted the possibilities and came up with
two answers. Either this was somebody from Stony
Man Farm or it was an enemy who had searched his
room, left a warning of some kind, or a bomb.

The second possibility had some merit to it.

One time before his Stony Man days, when Lyons
was still with the strike force, they had a major grand
jury investigation going on a narcotics syndicate.
Everything had looked good. The wiretaps were going
well, a couple of low-level enforcer types—"gunsels," in the jargon of the trade—had rolled over and
become informants.

Then, suddenly, without warning, things had gone
to shit. Or, as it was put later in the official reports,
the investigation "had undergone an abrupt turn-

around.'' That sounded better than "gone to shit" in a document that's going to be read by the head of the Justice Department.

The wiretaps had dried up. Known couriers changed their routes. An informant had dropped out of sight. The main targets, so-called respectable members of the community, suddenly became highly visible in the public eye. They did good works. They made showy contributions to charities.

How could someone be a Mafia hood if he supported the symphony?

It came to a finale one day when the agents returned to their secret base. In a safe house, specially rented in a quiet neighborhood, from which the investigation was coordinated. At that point in the case, the location of the safe house seemed to be the only thing that the Mafia hoods didn't know about.

So the agents thought, anyway.

When one of the agents opened the door, Lyons had realized instantly that even the safe house was blown.

He sensed the death.

Later, even Lyons didn't know how or why he had known.

Sure, the smell was there, but only if you consciously tried to find it. Certainly it had been nothing like some of the bloated corpses he had come across before, the cases when the gagging stench of death hit you like a wall and the flies were so thick in the Los Angeles summer heat that it sounded like a beehive.

But he sensed it nevertheless.

And, though he knew it wasn't necessary, that it was too late, Lyons had grabbed the lead agent by the arms and hauled him roughly outside. His Colt Python in his hand, Lyons had made a fast, skilled once-over of the safe house, the way he used to do as a street cop, until he found what he had somehow known would be there.

Their missing informant, the linchpin to the case.

He had been in the bedroom. He was actually in one of the beds, the covers pulled over him as if he were asleep. When the agents checked further, they found he had been thoroughly and messily disemboweled.

It had been an effective warning that the case was over, that everything had been blown sky-high.

It was not too long after that incident that Lyons had been cautiously approached by the man from Stony Man Farm.

Today Lyons recalled the incident as he stood outside the door to his hotel room. He weighed the possibilites and decided that whatever had been inside, it was not an ambush. It might be friend, or it might be a warning from a foe, similar to the safe house incident. But, in all probability, nothing immediately lethal waited for him inside.

Of course he could be wrong, the Ironman part of his mind said as he put the key in the door. And he knew that if he was, these could be the last seconds of his life.

He turned the knob and pushed the door open.

No bullets greeted him. No blinding flash erupted from the room.

For a moment he stood outside the room, behind the protection of the doorjamb, his hand on the specially modified .45 Government Model tucked inside his slacks under his shirt. Might as well not make it *too* easy for them, if I've guessed wrong, he thought.

He waited. Every nerve alive, he tried to sense if anybody was inside.

The bathroom and closet were immediately to his left when he stepped inside the doorway. Straight ahead he could see the dresser, the desk, the table, the TV. No sign of anybody. Nothing visible. Nothing audible.

Of course the main area of the room lay off to the left, beyond the bathroom, not visible from the doorway. That's where the king-size bed was.

Then he smelled it.

Just a hint, of course. Just the faintest trace of a scent he could never forget.

Lyons let his breath out in a long sigh. He stepped inside and pulled the door shut, in case some other motel guests appeared in the hallway and wondered what he was doing. Then he walked forward into the room, taking out the .45 as he did.

The scent was stronger inside. He glanced at the bed and saw the human shape under the covers.

The shape moved and spoke to him, a mocking, sultry voice. A voice which, like the scent of the perfume, Lyons knew would always take his breath away.

"Hello, sailor. You got twenty bucks?"

8

Lyons let out a slow, deep sigh of contentment.

It was his second sigh since the immediate festivities had terminated a few moments before. Then he adjusted his body so that most of his weight was supported by his elbows and forearms, and snuggled the side of his face next to her cheek.

She moved slightly beneath him.

"Too heavy?" he asked softly, supporting more of his weight on his arms.

"Not at all," she murmured.

"You sure?"

"Umm-hmm. Just getting more comfortable." Her sigh emulated his own, and she pulled him down on top of her.

They lay there still joined, drifting languidly in a hazy place of half-consciousness, located somewhere between sleep and wakening. With one hand she lightly stroked the back of his neck, first playing with his hair, then moving downward and tracing the contours of his trapezius muscles and shoulders with the tips of her fingers.

Almost as if he were outside himself, Lyons sensed his breathing become slower and deeper, and he marveled at the feeling of utter well-being that enveloped him.

He had known what—or who—he would find the moment he had caught the scent of her perfume after he pushed the door open. His deliberateness in walking inside after he realized who was waiting there came from two things. First, he wanted to prolong his delight that she would be there. Moreover, even though he knew it was juvenile, he had to admit part of it was a desire to look cool.

That perfume had always captivated him. He had never smelled that particular scent before he met her, and it was totally unique to her.

Like a fingerprint, he had once thought, realizing how unromantic the comparison would sound.

One time, when they had been spending a week together, he tried to find out what kind it was. His idea had been to give her a gift of something that complemented it. Maybe some body lotion, something that she might consider an indulgence to buy for herself.

Though he respected her privacy too much to ever look in her purse—even for a "good cause" like this— he watched her as she got dressed and put on her makeup one morning in the motel room. He hoped he'd see the bottle from which she got the scent, get the brand name and be in business.

The "surveillance" had proved to be a very pleasant activity in its own right, as it turned out. However, it also proved to be unrewarding in terms of his ultimate mission. She kept the perfume in a small travel bottle that bore no label or manufacturer's markings.

Finally he asked her. It was later that same trip, in fact, when they had gone out to dinner.

"What kind of perfume is that you're wearing, anyway?" he said, trying to keep his voice casual.

"What perfume?" she had responded, a hint of mischief in her voice.

"The perfume you have on."

"I don't have any perfume on. Must be from your other girlfriend."

"Very funny."

Lyons had grinned in what he hoped was an easy, casual manner. He knew—well, almost knew—she had to be pulling his leg. Still, he couldn't help wondering if maybe he had hugged somebody else recently, in a purely platonic, brother-sister fashion, of course.

It wasn't that he and FBI Agent Julie Harris were engaged or even had any specific agreement that foreclosed other relationships. Still, at the time that conversation had occurred, there had existed a sort of tacit understanding of exclusivity between them.

"Like if I catch you messing around, I'll cut it off and pickle it," she had once joked.

He affected to cringe. Then he responded that if she did that, it would cause an epidemic of broken hearts and mourning among the young women—and some not so young—all over America. It would be concentrated, of course, on the West Coast and would be particularly acute in Southern California.

Julie had not been overly amused by the jest.

Somehow sensing that, Lyons had sought to repair the damage. "Of course, that's all history," he added hastily. "Ancient history. Prehistoric in fact."

"I see." Her tone was still not exactly antifreeze. "How interesting," she said in a voice that told him that it was *not* interesting.

He put his arm around her. "Hey," he jived. "You know I'm just kidding. Besides, I wouldn't even be interested in anybody else. Hell, if you've got steak, hamburger holds no appeal. You know what I mean?"

"What an incredible compliment," she murmured with a smile. "Of course, you might find yourself running out of steak, especially if you keep talking about the chain of broken hearts."

"As I said, just kidding."

The hell of it was, he had often reflected, since Julie, he hadn't been interested in anybody else. Well, he was forced to amend to himself, not *really* interested in anybody else. Not seriously. Not for long, anyway. Say, not for more than a few hours at the most.

Sometimes, he reflected ruefully, a good deal less than that.

He and Julie had met on a case. A splinter group of Shiite Muslims had engaged the services of one of the deadliest assassins in the world, a man known only as Kadal. His mission had been to kill the delegates signing a treaty to end the bloodshed in the Middle East.

The FBI had a round-the-clock watch on Kadal, only it had gone bad. Kadal had discovered the bureau's informant and had returned her head to the FBI in a box. Enter Stony Man Farm. And enter Julie into the life of Carl Lyons.

An FBI agent herself, Julie had been attached to the team surveilling Kadal. When the decision was made to abandon the "due process" route and take Kadal out any way they could, Julie was dispatched to brief Able Team.

A cynical Carl Lyons, at the time firmly possessed of the belief that women had no place in any kind of police work, had suppressed a groan when he realized the bureau rep was a broa—, uh, woman. Almost immediately, however, he had realized his prejudice had been just that—prejudice. And like so many prejudices, it had been wrong.

Clearly she was more than a token female attached to a mission where she had no business being, just to satisfy some affirmative action committee somewhere.

She was one of the most competent operatives he had ever met.

Sure, she was beautiful. Thick, dark hair, which she wore in a radical style, compared to what the bureau normally went for. Lively dark eyes, a thousand miles deep, that could speak pages just by the way she looked at him.

That had been the start. The ending had been that they became lovers.

When the mission was concluded, Lyons and Julie had gone off together. They spent the next several weeks together, to heal their wounds, both physical and psychological. Since then, due largely to the demands of their respective schedules, they saw each other at infrequent intervals.

Each time they picked up where they had left off.

Each time, emotionally speaking, they went a little farther than the time before.

Today was no exception.

His heart had leaped when he realized who was inside his room. Still, he had forced a calm exterior. Pushing the door shut behind him, he had sauntered idly into the room.

When he got to where he could see the bed, he glanced over to confirm that he had been right. Then he had casually taken out his .45 and his wallet, setting them on the dresser as though he were coming home from a routine day at the office.

The scent of the perfume was stronger here. He reflected that she never had told him the name of it, way back when. Instead she had so skillfully put him on the defensive with the discussion about the broken hearts that he had forgotten to press her on the point.

Smart lady, he thought. Maybe too smart.

Today, when she spoke to him, as he entered the room, it was all he could do not to dive onto the bed, as if to smother himself in her arms, her scents, her love.

He didn't, though.

"Hi, babe. When did you get into town?" he said offhandedly.

Julie was more than equal to the challenge. "A couple of days ago. Week maybe." Her voice was even more casual than his had been, if that was possible.

"I'm glad you dropped by."

"Yeah. I looked up a few old friends, guys, mainly. Then when I heard you were in town, I figured I might as well look you up, too."

"After only a week, too," he responded. "Hell, I'm flattered, you know?"

She shrugged. "Things are slow."

He sensed the casual game was something he couldn't win, not this time, anyway. Still, he was determined not to throw in the towel. "So, where've you been, lately?"

"Seattle."

"Business?"

"Yeah."

"How was the weather?"

"Not too great. It rained." She pretended to stifle a yawn.

Lyons looked at her in sheer delight. She was in the bed, covers pulled up around her. Beneath the imitation boredom a delicious malice danced in her eyes. He glanced around the room.

No sign of her clothes.

He felt the heat in his groin. Still keeping his voice casual—which had become something of a struggle now—he spoke in a careless tone. "You, uh, wearing anything under there?"

"Why, gee, I don't know." She lifted the covers and peered beneath them for several moments. Lyons, from his position, couldn't see, which only served to intensify his ardor.

"Well?"

Julie let the sheet fall back across her body. "Nope. Doesn't look like it, anyway." She paused for a moment, then continued. "Which makes you a really rude bastard, standing there with all your clothes on and a lump in your pants, cross-examining me like that."

Not that any invitation had been necessary, but Lyons hesitated no longer.

Unlike Julie's clothes—which he later discovered she had folded and placed carefully under the bed, just so he wouldn't see them lying around somewhere—Lyons's own garments ended up scattered all over the room as he yanked them from his body.

Her skin felt white-hot against his, her breath warm and sweet. The sheets made a pleasing contrast, cool and coarse. They touched and caressed and teased, then joined in a rising tide of passion that escalated steeply until it ended for both of them in a shared rush of ecstacy.

Much later, still lying on her, Lyons stirred at last. Rolling onto his side, he saw her watching him solemnly.

"How have you been, love?" Her voice was soft.

"I'm fine, now."

"Objection—nonresponsive to the question."

"Jesus," he said, grinning. "Spare me the courtroom crap. How did you ever get through the security to find me, anyway?" He was thinking about the elaborate veil of secrecy that Brognola had created for the entire Stony Man concept.

"It wasn't easy."

"Good. I hope not." When she didn't elaborate he pressed the issue. "So how did you do it?"

"I called up Hal and asked him where you were."

Lyons gave that one some thought.

One didn't just look in the Yellow Pages for Stony Man's number. It wasn't listed in any directory of the U.S. Government, not even in the massive computer-generated compendium that had area codes, numbers and extensions for virtually every desk of every agency that existed.

"Where'd you get the number?"

She looked at him with more than a trace of irritation. "It was written on the wall of the ladies' room at the FBI headquarters. 'For a good time, call the Ironman at…' How do you think I got it, for God's sake? I'm not exactly some flunky off the streets, you know."

"I know," he responded. "I didn't mean to sound patronizing. Sorry."

"I'm sorry, too," she said, her voice softening. Then she giggled. "You are still the Ironman, Carl. At least in one respect, anyway."

"What respect is that?" he teased.

"You know."

"I just want to hear you say it."

"All right. In the respect that I just experienced."

"Thank you, ma'am. All glowing testimonials greatly appreciated. Even if I did have to haul them out of you by pliars."

"You're welcome."

He paused for a moment. "Actually, I guess I was trying to inquire—with a certain degree of diplomacy—whether your arrival here had any business aspects to it or whether it was strictly pleasure."

"You're a suspicious bastard, aren't you?"

"Just thought I'd ask."

"Well, if you must know, it was all my idea. All pleasure, and no, I really wasn't here a week before I looked you up. I came here straight from the airport, if you must know."

He smiled and relaxed a little. "Thanks."

"And now, if you don't mind, I'd rather stop playing "twenty questions."

Her hands, which had been lightly tracing designs on his chest, wandered downward along his frame. "Think you're up to it?" she teased.

"Lady, you're asking a lot from an old guy."

"I think you've got it in you."

"Animal," Lyons muttered in mock disgust. "Just a sex animal." And then Lyons grinned.

9

"Damn."

The oath didn't come from Lyons but from Julie. It was a hundredfold too mild to be the way Lyons wanted to express himself at that moment.

He considered letting the phone ring itself out.

Just ignore it, in other words.

But, Ironman or not—Julie had earned herself five hundred points with that compliment—he knew it would seriously, and perhaps terminally, impair his amorous abilities if he was to try to ignore a ringing telephone.

Especially this phone. As he looked at it in dismay, Lyons saw it was the most businesslike of telephones, a sturdy-looking amber contrivance with what had to be the loudest and most obnoxious ringer in the Southern California area.

The cheap wood nightstand didn't help, of course.

Lyons gritted his teeth. How could one little bell be so noisy?

Well, take one loud, field-grade telephone. Install a heavy-duty ringer in it—none of those wimpy bells in this baby—then crank the volume up high. Finally, set it on the hard, flat, sound-amplifying surface of a Formica motel nightstand. Then see how easy it is to concentrate on other matters at hand, even if they are very pleasant matters.

Other possibilites appeared fleetingly in his mind. Though they all sounded attractive in one respect or another, he dismissed each one in turn.

One option was to yank the telephone out by the roots. *Hey, Ironman, bet you can't make a left hook with it into the trash can in the far corner of the room. Oh, yeah? Wanna bet? Watch this....*

Or, see if he could throw it through the safety-glass window of the motel. These high-rise jobs were hermetically sealed, and the glass was supposed to be tough enough to keep people from falling out. Let's see how good they were on phones.

Then another idea occurred to him. It sounded good, damn good, in fact.

Shoot it. Just blow the bastard away. Shoot the shit out of it. Obnoxious bell or not, that would shut the goddamn thing up.

Lyons carried high-velocity silver-tips in the .45 Government Model. The weapon was the basic unit except for certain tuning and smoothing improvements added by John "Cowboy" Kissinger, the master weaponsmith at Stony Man Farm.

One of Kissinger's key improvements included a new spring in the clip. It enabled the weapon to hold one more round than the factory mechanism.

The spring was located beneath the "floor-plate," which went below the ammo and pushed it upward to be fed into the breach. The original standard issue spring could only be compressed enough to hold seven rounds in the magazine, plus one in the chamber, of course.

The new spring was more compressible yet still reliable. As a result the weapon now held eight in the magazine, along with the one in the chamber.

Nine rounds total.

Nine rounds, Lyons reflected, would certainly silence the clamoring telephone. Plus there would be a certain gut-level satisfaction about having blasted the hell out of it.

That plan had its own drawbacks, however.

Some busybody in an adjoining room might not realize that all Lyons wanted was a little peace and quiet, so he could make love to his girlfriend. The busybody would probably call the front desk and complain. Then the motel management and security force would probably get all stuffy about it. They'd start pounding on the door, and that would be nearly as disruptive as the phone itself.

Besides, he had left the damn gun clear across the room, on the dresser.

Lyons had run out of ideas. With a muttered oath, he leaned over to answer the jangling phone.

"Ohh," Julie complained in good-natured protest.

Then a minor inspiration struck. Like most good plans, it was the simplest one of all. He just picked up the receiver and dropped it down on the cradle again. It effectively severed the connection.

"Presto!" he said with a smile. "Now you hear it, now you don't. And now, where were we?"

Thirty seconds later it rang again. With a sigh Lyons pushed himself off Julie and crawled to where he could sit on the edge of the bed. The "iron" in Ironman—that Julie had so recently commented upon—subsided completely.

He reached for the telephone and answered it.

"Linguine-man here," he said, gazing down at the dear departed. Then, trying to be good-natured, he turned and rolled his eyes at Julie. "And this better not be just the Avon lady, or Avon's going to be wiped out."

The hollow sound of long-distance wires—actually radio or microwaves, these days, he thought—greeted him. So did the booming, cheerful voice of Hal Brognola, chief of operations at Stony Man Farm.

"Carl! Is that you?"

"Yeah." He sighed in resignation. "It's me."

"Carl. What's going on? Are you drunk, Ironman? What's up with you, buddy?"

Julie could hear Brognola's hearty voice from the receiver, even where she lay. She giggled.

"Tell him nothing's up, not now, anyway," she whispered. Before Lyons could respond, though, Brognola went on.

"I hope I didn't interrupt anything, but it seemed better me than Blancanales."

"What do you mean?"

Lyons could picture the Stony Man chief, leaning back in the swivel chair in his office. He would have the inevitable cigar in hand and, on the desk, a stained porcelain coffee mug half filled with cold coffee. Somewhere nearby would be the Bear himself, Aaron Kurtzman, computer and intelligence whiz of the operation.

Kurtzman, the technical genius, and Brognola, the strategist. Together, they would plot and direct the moves of the Stony Man units, like two masterminds deciding where to move the knight or rook in some deadly international chess match.

Lyons and the others were pieces on the board. They knew it. They accepted it. And, moreover, they liked it.

"Blancanales will ETA there in approximately an hour. He'll have something for you. After you read it, make contact with me."

"We have a mission?"

"After you've read it," Brognola repeated, "and talked to Blancanales, call me."

"Does this have anything to do with Danny Forbes?" Lyons asked bluntly.

Brognola hesitated just long enough, or a fraction of a second too long, Lyons thought.

"Who?"

In all the years Lyons had known his chief, this was one of the first times he had ever appeared at a loss for words. And also one of the first times since they had known each other that Lyons stepped out of rank.

"Come off it, Hal. This is me. Lyons. Not some...", he groped for words, then borrowed the phrase from Julie, "flunky off the streets, for God's sake."

"What do you know about Danny Forbes?" Brognola's voice was stiff, a touch angry.

"You know what I know about him from the past," Lyons retorted. "It's all on the record."

"And recently?" pursued the Stony Man chief. "How did you happen to mention his name just now?"

"I've just come from the National City Police Department. I've spent a fucking delightful hour looking at pictures of that pitiful bastard with his skull popped and his brains squeezed out by the jaws of the biggest goddamn vise in the world.'' Behind him, Julie's eyes narrowed, but Lyons ignored it.

''You're sure?'' Brognola asked softly. ''It *was* Danny, then? A positive ID?''

Lyons drew a long, slow breath.

So there had been a mission behind all this, after all. And it had been tied to Danny Forbes. And if the logic held up—and he knew beyond doubt it would—the judge was tied in to it, also.

The Ironman supposed he should have been gratified. After all, he had guessed right all the way around.

He had wondered if something was up. Then, with only the barest of clues, he had used his innate abilities to correctly infer that the body in the Excedrin case—shit, he was doing it, too—might be involved. Well, he thought, to be more accurate, it was not only his innate abilities. It was also a lot of experience in the secret-agent commando business, in which survival often depended on the ability to make that kind of deduction accurately.

Aloud, he cleared his throat and said, ''Yeah. It was Danny.'' His voice sounded rusty, even to himself.

''No question about it?''

''For chrissakes, Hal, I recruited him and worked with him for over two years. I recognized him in the pictures.'' Even if his head would now fit in a shoe box, as Grogan had suggested.

''How did you happen to end up checking in on that situation, anyway?'' the Stony Man chief asked after a moment.

"It's a long story. Basically, a couple of good guesses, that's all."

"No breach of security?"

"No."

Brognola was silent for several moments. When he spoke again, his tone had a softer quality to it. "All right, Lyons. When Blancanales gets there, let him brief you. Then make contact here."

"Ten-four." Lyons's voice made an irritated acknowledgment of the directive.

"Oh, yes. We've got a flight for you this evening. Reservations made, tickets prepaid. Yours will be under the name Charlie Leanord. The Politician is booked under the name of Balcazar. Destination, Miami."

"Miami?"

"Yes. Miami. I want you in place there by tomorrow. So you'll be flying there late tonight. The flights suck, you'll be arriving there at 0300 Miami time, but that's the way it is."

"Just me and Blanc?"

"Gadgets will meet you there. He should be en route right now, as a matter of fact."

"What's going down in Miami?"

"I'll brief you when you get there." Brognola's voice was curt.

"Any other details you'd care to share with me?" Lyons inquired with heavy sarcasm. He was by now convinced beyond any doubt that Danny Forbes represented the first step on a trail that would lead to the Florida cocaine trade.

"Look. I've got my reasons for playing this so close to the vest, Carl. As the man in the field, you understand that, I'm sure."

His voice had a note of conciliation to it, almost like the guy was apologizing, Lyons thought.

It suddenly occurred to Lyons that maybe he had been acting like a baby. As chief, Brognola had no obligation to explain any of his orders or why he did what he did. The fact that Brognola made mention of this, though, was an indication of how much he thought of Lyons, that he was willing to go the extra mile for the benefit of the field man.

Snap out of it, Ironman, he told himself. Quit being a fucking prima donna.

He forced a smile, forgetting that of course Hal couldn't see it over the phone. "Orders is orders, guy. I know that. You're the brains, I'm the brawn. Sorry I was testy."

"No sweat." His voice carried the message that the subject was closed. "One other thing, Lyons."

"Yeah?"

"I took the liberty of telling your, uh, friend Agent Harris where to find you. It seems reasonable to expect she may be showing up on your doorstep."

Lyons looked over his shoulder at Julie, lying on the bed, a sheet wrapped around her. She saw him and gave him a questioning look. He winked, and she made an exaggerated pantomime of pulling the sheet lower to reveal the upper swell of her breasts.

"Thanks, Hal," he said into the phone. "You know how these broads are...." He used that term deliberately, to tease Julie, knowing how much she hated it.

His reward was a swift and solid kick to his bare back, right in the vicinity of his kidney.

On the other end of the line, Brognola's laugh boomed out heartily. "Well, I just thought I'd warn you. I figured that if you didn't want to see her, you could skate out of there before she arrived. She'd just figure you'd moved on, if that's what you want."

Too late, Lyons realized that his chief's resonant voice could easily be heard by Julie and probably by the people in the next room, for that matter.

A gasp of outrage—deliberately accentuated for effect, he knew—told him that she had, in fact, tapped in on Brognola's words.

The second kick was even more solid and well placed than the first one.

Lyons grunted and tried to move, still naked, out of range.

"Yeah, Chief. Thanks a lot," he said hastily. "That won't be necessary, though. Look. I'll call you as soon as I talk to the Politician. Okay? See you around, Hal."

He broke the connection and turned to Julie. She was sitting up against the headboard, filing her fingernails. She had the sheets and blanket and bedspread pulled up tightly around her body, clamped into place by her arms.

Despite the kick, which had been in the form of good-natured kidding, Lyons could tell that her feelings were really hurt on this one.

"Hey, baby," he said softly.

She turned to Lyons with an icy indifference. "And how is good old Hal?"

"Great. Blancanales is coming over. Something about a mission, maybe."

"That's fine. I'll get out of your hair."

"You don't have to do that."

"It's no trouble, really."

Lyons looked at her in real exasperation. "Look, Julie. *I* didn't say that stuff. The chief did. Besides, that's just bullshit man talk. I wouldn't cut out on you. Hell, you know I love to see you."

"Oh? Is that so?"

"Yes, that's so."

"How do I know that his business with Blancanales isn't another one of your little man-talk schemes?"

"It isn't."

She ignored him. "Maybe you have a playbook. Somebody calls the signals, and everybody knows what roles to take." She imitated a quarterback in a football game. "'Down. Set. Ninety-nine right,' or something. And then you all cover for each other."

"It's not like that. Hell, Julie, I love to see you. And you know it," he added lamely.

She didn't respond.

"Hell, I don't just love to see you. In fact, I love you, you know?"

10

The room felt different somehow. Tension hung in the air. It was as if the atmosphere had been changed by Lyons's awkward pronouncement.

Julie turned slowly and looked in his direction. For many long moments she gazed at him without speaking. Then finally she broke the silence, her voice flat and toneless.

"That's not necessary, Carl."

Puzzled, he responded. "It's what I feel. I'm just not too good at saying it, I guess."

She looked quickly away from him. When she spoke again, her voice was uncharacteristically harsh.

"Don't ever lie to me, you bastard."

"What?" Amazement showed in his voice.

"I don't care what you feel like you ought to say. Just don't ever lie to me. Especially not to save my feelings. I'm a big girl, goddamn it, and I can't stand to be patronized."

Lyons looked at her, stunned.

Of all the possible reactions he might have imagined—had he considered them before making his spontaneous utterance—this was not one of them. His face burned with the anger and humiliation of rejection. He felt slightly queasy, like he'd taken a boot in the guts.

He stared at her, wondering if he had really heard her say that or if it might be some sort of psychotic fiction.

She still sat with her back against the headboard, arms hugging the bedclothes against her abdomen. Her head was turned resolutely away from him, so that she was facing the opposite direction. Her body shook as if she were crying.

Fuck, he thought, what had he done? What raw nerve had he touched, what bloody wound exposed?

Lyons was torn, his mind drawn and quartered in a brutal emotional conflict. Part of him wanted to go to her, to comfort her, to hold her. He'd take it back. He's say whatever she wanted to make her not hurt. He'd...

Then he realized that would be doing exactly what she asked him not to do. In addition, his awkwardly blurted statement happened to be true.

It wasn't something he just said for convenience or to get into her pants. It was the truth.

The other part of him wanted to lash out, to defend himself by attacking her.

Hurt and anger welled up. To hell with you, he thought. I'm not a bad guy, and I meant what I was saying. You bitch, do you think you're just some piece of ass to me? I'm not like that, goddamn you....

Sure, I'm older than you are. Sure, I've been married and divorced, sure I'm not perfect. But I treat you nice, partly because I'm a good guy—I'd treat any woman that way—but also because I love you. And if that's not good enough for you, hell, if *I'm* not good enough for you, then fuck you, I'm outta here.

Half of him said stay, talk to her. The other half said split, get out of there.

The latter part won.

Without a word Lyons collected his clothes and got dressed. Seething in anger, slow-burn all the way, he glanced around the room, deliberately avoiding looking at Julie.

Most of his stuff was already packed, at least whatever was out in the main part of the room. A couple of shirts were hanging in the closet; a small bundle of dirty clothes lay on the floor.

He yanked the shirts from the hangers and jammed them into his roll bag. Bending over, he retrieved the dirty laundry and did likewise. Then he checked the bathroom. Most of his toiletries—shaving lather, the twin-blade razor, after-shave and deodorant—were there, still on the counter by the sink.

He thought about packing them, then said to hell with it.

A plastic wastebasket sat on the floor, next to the toilet. He seized it and held it next to the edge of the counter by the sink. Using his forearm, he swept the toiletries off the counter into the trash container, then dropped it to the floor.

He stalked into the room and glanced around.

Julie lay on her side, legs drawn up into a fetal position, her back to him, the covers tightly wrapped around her.

His .45 still lay on the dresser. He picked it up and jammed it into his belt, then ran the zipper of his bag shut. Then, grabbing it, he strode to the door, knowing he was being a jerk but unwilling to put it right.

Besides, he thought, it was her fault.

He considered throwing a twenty at her and then felt ashamed that he had even thought of it. The "hey, sailor, got twenty bucks," line was from an episode he had once told her, an anecdote from his cop days. She had laughed and laughed, the way only she could, a dark, vital explosion of mirth, and the phrase had found its way into their intimacy ever since.

To use it to strike out at her, even now, would be to cheapen everything they had shared.

At the door he turned to her.

"For what it's worth," he said harshly, "it happened to be the truth."

He turned and strode out the door, resisting the temptation to slam it. With every step, he listened, hoping—praying—he would hear her voice, calling him back.

No such luck.

He reached the elevator at the end of the hall. Angrily he jabbed the call button. Moments later the door opened, and Blancanales stepped out.

Rosario Blancanales, aka "the Politician."

The son of illegal immigrants who had crawled under the fence from Mexico to the U.S. in the 1950s, he was one of the three core members of Able Team. He was also probably Lyons's best friend.

He had spent his childhood in the Latino community of east Los Angeles and the California-Mexico border town of San Ysidro, just south of San Diego. His parents had been hardworking people, imbued of the work ethic that made so many immigrants view America as the promised land, a place of freedom and the chance to be something worth being.

As a child, Blancanales had chafed under the strictures of his parents' code of hard work and saving. Still, he was unable to shed his own feelings of responsibility to the family. The result was that he worked in the family restaurants by day, and by night he prowled the streets as part of a youth gang.

He still carried some of the scars to prove it.

It had been a slightly schizophrenic existence. The strong, restless young man he had become was torn between his sense of duty and an unquenchable thirst for action.

Then came Vietnam.

Sergeant Barry Sadler's "Ballad of the Green Berets" hit the top of the charts. Students in Berkeley fought the cops and flattened chain link fences by the sheer weight of their bodies. Some young people fried their brains on chemicals, turning on, tuning in and dropping out, while others the same age saw their blood flow into the muddy soil of Southeast Asia.

For the young Blancanales the answer gradually emerged out of the mist. It proved to be a way to discharge both his sense of duty and to get all the action he ever wanted and then some.

The moment he made the decision to enlist in the U.S. Army, Blancanales knew beyond any doubt that he had done the right thing.

Boot camp. Jump school. And later, Jungle Warfare School. He won the coveted Green Beret.

In Vietnam he had established himself as a natural leader. His quick, easy smile—the trademark that would later lead to his nickname, the Politician—and his ability to make just the right quip at just the right time were combined with an utter lack of fear in the young soldier. Though he generally shunned positions of formal leadership, he became one of those quiet anchors of courage that inspires others simply by his own willingness to face whatever might be ahead.

Young men who didn't even know his name would see him and would be inspired by· him. Frightened boys would remember his fatalistic courage and carry that image with them on nerve-stretching patrols and into bloody firefights.

In Vietnam, he met Mack Bolan, who was engaged in a secret intelligence effort. He, too, had been impressed by the young Politician.

The two men carried out that mission and, in ensuing months, several others. Many of those would not normally have involved the Politician's unit; all of them were for volunteers only.

In all of them, Bolan had pulled the strings necessary to allow Blancanales to be given the chance to "volunteer."

Blancanales did, in fact, volunteer whenever it was Bolan at the helm. And it had been a real "volunteer," not the standard military "you *will* volunteer."

It was an alliance that led Blancanales to join in Bolan's subsequent "war" against the Mafia, and after that to become an integral part of the Stony Man operation.

Today, in his mid-thirties, the Politician was just that.

Lyons was the unofficial leader of Able Team, and Blancanales preferred it that way. And the same calm courage, added to his ready charm, continued to serve him as unfailingly as it had in the jungles and rice paddies.

Physically Blancanales was in perhaps the best shape of his life. Well, make that partly true, he would have corrected had he been asked. Though still possessed of incredible powers of endurance, he could remember a time, back when he was lighter—and younger—when it felt easier to run ten miles than it did these days.

It had its compensation, though, he would probably add with a wink. These days he was stronger, and in terms of his abilities at making love...

Medium height, he had a thin-skinned and dense musculature that somehow belied his stocky frame. His dark complexion and aquiline features made him handsome and lent a quality of mystery to him. This was accentuated by prematurely gray hair and a forehead that had become deeply lined, a sign perhaps that his outward manifestation of easy courage had not been as automatic as he made it seem.

"Yo, Ironman," Blancanales said as he and Lyons found themselves face-to-face in the door of the elevator. "You checking out?"

"Yeah." The response was curt.

The Politician shrugged and stepped back into the elevator. He knew enough to see that Lyons was in no mood to be questioned and would speak when he wanted to speak.

They went to the checkout window at the front desk. Lyons paid for the room, which included that night, since it was already early afternoon. He used cash, then turned to Blancanales and picked up his suitcase.

"Let's go."

"Where to?"

"Airport. Chief says we're going to Miami."

"When?"

"Tonight."

"Just us?"

"Gadgets is supposed to meet us there or join us there or something."

"*Bueno.*" Blancanales shrugged. It occurred to him that "tonight" was still some time off. Still, it might be possible to advance the flights, so he said nothing. Ten minutes later, they were in Lyons's rental car and were en route to San Diego's Lindburgh Field.

Finally Lyons broke his self-imposed silence.

"Sorry, partner."

"What for?" Both men knew the Politician's response was actually saying not to worry about it.

"For being such a dick just now."

"Something on your mind, Ironman?"

Lyons made a disgusted sound. "Ahh, no big deal. Usual bullshit whenever you let some woman get under your skin a little. That's all."

"Julie?" the Politician inquired sympathetically. Lyons shrugged, which was answer enough.

"So," Lyons said abruptly, changing the subject with all the subtlety of a knock on the side of the head, "what's the story from Brognola?"

"What has he already told you, amigo?"

"Not much. That you would be showing up. That you had something for me to read. That after I read it I should make contact with the Farm."

"That's it?"

"That's it."

Blancanales took a deep breath. "Here's how it shakes down, Homes."

The word "Homes" was a short form of "Home-boys," a popular term with street gangs.

A Home-boy was a fellow gang member, somebody who actually belonged to the same gang. But it meant more than just that. The term carried meanings of loyalty and friendship and a willingness to defend the other person, right or wrong—all the things that belonging to a gang meant.

"If the dude's one of your Home-boys, mon," Blancanales had explained, imitating a hoarse, guttural, street-Mexican way of speaking, "it means you 'back his play,' you know? You gotta back the dude up, right or wrong, mon."

Recently he and Lyons and Gadgets had taken to using the word on occasion, when addressing each other. Partly it was an attempt to recognize the humor and humanity of the streets. It sounded cool, so to speak. But an undeniable part of its appeal involved the notions of loyalty the term brought to mind.

Lyons, his anger beginning to abate, recognized what Blancanales was trying to do and acknowledged it by using the term himself. "Yeah, Homes?"

The Politician grinned, then responded.

"Most of this is guesswork, but here's what I think is up. Some guy who was an informant on a big cocaine case the Feds had put together in Florida dropped out of sight. They think the guy's been iced.

The case is set to go to trial, and they can't do it without him.''

Lyons shot a sidelong glance at his partner. It was apparent that he, too, hadn't been given much information.

"That's it?" he inquired. "That's all they told you."

"*Sí*, amigo."

"So where do we fit in?"

Blancanales winked. "I think we are to succeed where others have failed."

"You mean go in and take care of the crooks? Ice the icers, so to speak?" Lyons thought for a moment. "Not that I mind of course, but I'm surprised they would just want us to knock off some asshole who beat the rap by killing a snitch."

"Does the idea offend you, Ironman?"

"Not in the slightest. But there's got to be something more to it than just some archcriminal might walk."

"Walk?" inquired the Politician, not understanding the term.

"Beat the rap. Walk on the case. Get set free." Lyons grimaced. "No," he repeated, "I don't mind at all. Still, Brognola is a staunch supporter of the constitution."

"I agree."

Lyons went on. "Not to mention Bolan—hell, he makes the President look like a socialist in that regard. And none of them, including the man in the White House, would go for knocking off some crook just because some stupid judges created some stupid rules that let the guy off."

"You have a point, amigo."

"There's got to be more to it." Lyons took the off ramp for the rental car return. "What did the chief give you to give to me, anyway?"

"A letter. It's for you. It came from the Department of Justice. Some majordomo there delivered it personally to Brognola. It has something to do with our mission."

Lyons parked the car in the return lane. Taking out the rental agreement from the glove box, he logged the mileage and how full the tank was on the appropriate spaces on the form, then dropped it in the slot for speedy return.

"Let's see if we can get our flight moved up; then I'll read it. We'll call him from Miami."

Blancanales wrinkled his brow. "I'm not too sure that's what he had in mind, Ironman. I believe he wanted you to read it, then call him from here."

"He didn't say that." Lyons strode toward the ticket counter. "Hell, he didn't say much of anything, come to think of it."

"He was being very secretive," admitted the Politician.

"Yep. So he can't very well complain if we have to guess as to exactly what he wanted, can he, Homes?"

A grin split Blancanales's face. He nodded slowly. "You're right, Homes. Miami it is."

The two men gave each other the high-five and walked toward the ticket counter. Lyons tried not to think about the beautiful woman with the dark hair.

It wasn't easy. He wondered if it would ever get any easier.

Time alone would tell.

11

Forty minutes later they were airborne.

Delta, it turned out, had a flight from San Diego to Miami, with one stop in between, scheduled to depart at 3:38, San Diego time. They would arrive in Miami shortly before midnight, given the three-hour time difference.

One end of the continent to the other in a matter of a few hours, Lyons thought. Lower left corner to lower right corner, as you faced the map.

Amazing.

The flight had vacant seats, and the two men had no difficulty in advancing their reservations from the later flight that Brognola—or Kurtzman, actually—had booked.

Lyons deliberately postponed reading the missive brought by Blancanales until the flight got under way. There was a peculiar sort of privacy about flying, even on a crowded flight. He wanted to wait for that privacy before getting into the letter. And in fact, it worked; they ended up having a short row of three seats to themselves.

There was another reason for putting it off, as well.

He knew that once he had read the letter, there would be no way to avoid thinking about Julie. But until then he could use it to keep at bay the queasy feeling. So he postponed reading the letter and would do so a couple of more times, a half hour at a time. Wondering what was in it helped force Julie out of his mind, and the prospect of finally reading the letter would be like a reward for holding out so long.

It was, he reflected, similar to a wounded man putting off the next shot of painkiller, something he was not altogether unfamiliar with.

The jet took off over the Pacific, northwest, then made a long sweeping turn to begin its journey east. The evening rushed toward them, an accelerated twilight caused by flying away from the setting sun.

Then it was time.

He nudged Blancanales. "You got that letter or whatever the chief wanted me to read?"

"*Sí*, amigo."

"Might as well take a look at it, I guess."

Wordlessly the Politician handed the paper over. He knew what it said; Brognola had shown the letter to him. Still, he also had known not to try to discuss its contents until Lyons had read it and was ready to talk.

What Lyons was given was a photocopy of a handwritten letter, several pages long.

The original had evidently been written on standard notebook paper. Lyons could see the three circles along the left edge where the copier had picked up the binder holes.

He immediately recognized the handwriting, of course. For an instant the distorted features of Danny Forbes, his face crushed by the vise, surged in his mind.

Danny Forbes.

A sucker who had never been given an even break, until Lyons came along. A many-time loser, until the Ironman had yanked him, fighting all the way, out of the pits.

Maybe that was why it had hit him so hard. In a way, he had helped in the birth of the Danny Forbes who died in that warehouse.

And maybe if he hadn't left the strike force... Whoa, Ironman, you can't direct your own life around the needs of an ex-con coke dealer turned snitch.

Dear Mr. Lyons:
I'm sorry to have to be writing you like this. But I got no place to turn to. I got a bunch of guys that are trying to get me, and the witness protection program isn't helping any.

I made this big case against the biggest dealer in Miami. A guy named Ramon Lucero. Well, everybody on the streets knows him, knows he's the MAN behind it all. Its a big case Mr. Lyons. Like you and me used to do. I got a buy into some low guy who sold me an ounce. Then I got more buys for more C, and then I set up a sale for over eleven pounds.

Lyons read between the lines, drawing on his background in the narcotics enforcement business.

What Danny had described sounded like a classic narcotics investigation. A confidential informant, acting undercover of course, would make a small buy, sometimes several small buys, to be exact.

Gradually the dealer would come to trust the buyer. The informant would demonstrate his reliability. He did this in large part by virtue of the fact that time would go on, and there would be no arrest behind the sales.

Maybe the CI would prove his reliability further by using some of the drug in the presence of the dealer. Prosecutors, judges and juries had a fit with that. The peaceful naive idiots who judged the suspect's guilt tended to get real self-righteous if an informant had to admit he'd snorted a line or two as part of the deal.

Sounds like entrapment, juries and defense attorneys would say.

Sure. Like the case of some international businessman, a guy who moved and grooved in the circles of high finance and commerce, claiming he was entrapped into setting up a major narcotics deal. Yet juries bought that crap all the time.

Hell, who but another crook would a crooked dealer trust? "When the play is cast in hell, you can't expect angels as actors and actresses."

At any rate, then the buys would increase until a major deal could be consummated. And eleven pounds—probably five kilos, thought Lyons, which would be slightly over eleven—was a major deal.

The public read so much in the press about huge megaweights being seized they tended to lose perspective. But a five-kilo deal was big. Damn big. Easily enough to get you real dead if the seller thought you were setting him up.

Good work, Danny, thought Lyons. You were batting in the big leagues for sure.

He read on.

Not me to buy it you understand. They'd know it was too heavy for me. But me introducing another guy who was suppose to be a big dealer from Vegas. Only he was really an agent, a Feebie you know.

This Feebie he was good. Not as good as you, like when we did those bikers on that crystal thing that time. We fooled those guys solid, didn't we Mr. Lyons? Anyway this guy wasn't like most FBI guys. Lot of them are real smart but can't talk to dealers and shit. And they treat the informant like dirt, like some kind of garbage. Which you never did to me, even though I was not as good as you.

This guy is gonna be the big dealer from Vegas, see. I make the intro. We get the deal set down. Gonna go down next night.

Only they changed it on us. Lucero did. He sent a couple a guys to find me, and they brought me to him. Blindfolded me and shit. Don't you see Mr. Lyons? I was face-to-face with the MAN, just me and his men and him. And the MAN, he told me they were changing the plans and shit, and there had better be no fuck-ups or I'd end up with my mouth shut for good.

The Feebie, the good one, wasn't with me of course. The deal was supposed to be with some guy that worked for Lucero. So I'm the only guy who can pin it on L, and the prosecutor told me they weren't gonna go against Lucero because there wasn't any other evidence. No corroboration, besides my word. He said they weren't gonna go and nobody would ever know I could of fingered the MAN, so I didn't have anything to worry about.

As he read Lyons could see evidence of pressure that Danny Forbes had been under. And Lyons noticed Danny's sentences became longer and seemed hastily written.

Probably fear, he suspected. The emotions would be showing through as he got to the bad parts, the place where he got burned, where some prosecutor or some judge had pissed backward and ordered his identity revealed.

Danny would have good reason to be afraid, Lyons knew. If a drug kingpin learned or even believed, true or not, that somebody was setting him up, there could only be one response.

Some observers characterized that kind of rubout as a simple business decision, nothing personal, as though that showed how evil the drug business was. Lyons knew better. It was business, sure, but it was more than that. A guy like Lucero would certainly not hesitate to order such a hit, but it would be personal as well as business.

"Get that bastard," he would say, "I'll teach them to fuck with *me*. And when you do, make it hurt. I want the word to get out."

Lyons read on, aware as only an insider in the world of major drugs could be of what Danny would have been going through.

Mr. Lyons I believed those guys. They weren't as good as you, but I didn't think they would lie to me and hang me out to dry and shit. Next thing I know they got an indictment against Lucero and the judge says my identity has to be released. So they give me a new name, change all the records and shit and put me in the witness protection program. Only Lucero put the word out on the streets, and there was fifty thousand on my head and every dirt bag on the streets was looking for me.

The MAN Lucero has this guy who does the protection for him. A Cuban called Lalo, a real mean bastard. Mr. Lyons, I knew about Lalo before we even did this buy, and he's the meanest dude alive in the world. He's tall for a Cuban asshole, maybe not quite six feet but almost. Strong. Real strong. Veins and shit all over his muscles, but lean, you know. He likes to hurt people. They say one time he skinned an entire man alive, actually skinned the poor bastard so he would feel it and then dropped him into the ocean off the Keys in the saltwater and shit. And they did it because the guy had burned them. Word in Little Havana is, Lalo's got bad magic but I don't buy that shit.

Lyons remembered the description in McMurray's report about the Cuban whom he took to be the leader. Taller than the others, lean, muscular, the guy who "moved very quickly" when the shooting started. He would also be a man who would put a man's head in a vise and tighten it.

"Bad magic," pondered the Ironman.

Well, maybe. And then again, maybe not. But incidents such as that certainly did lend credence to the theory that evil was an actual, viable force in the world, rather than just the absence of good.

Lyons knew he'd see how bad his magic was.

He turned to the next page and continued reading.

A guy told me Lalo was after me. Lalo has an army of guys, mostly Cubans, that he is the leader of, and they have guns and grenades and rockets and shit that Lucero, the MAN, gets for them, and, Mr. Lyons, if that Lalo is coming after me I might as well blow my own brains out because that's better than him getting me. So I told the Feebie that Lalo was after me and Mr. Lyons he was good to me, he got me into the big witness program but it didn't work. Lalo found out somehow. The word on the streets is the MAN Lucero has some guy in the Justice Department that feeds him stuff, and that guy told him about my new name and everything. So I'm on the run, Mr. Lyons, and I don't know who to go to besides you. No disrespect, Mr. Lyons, sir, but be real careful if you can help me I don't even know if you could take Lalo even though you are the Ironman. That Lalo is mean, and I believe if there's such a thing as bad magic he has got it.

I need your help Mr. Lyons. I'm going to California, I think, and will be in Dago in two weeks. I'll be hiding out, but I'll check the paper every day. If you can help me, put an ad in the personals that says Ironman and your phone no. I'll call you.

Mr. Lyons, I'm scared. This guy Lalo scares me. I'm not proud to say it. I hope you can help me, but if you can't I understand. You were always fair with me, and I appreciate that.

Signed your friend
D. F.

Lyons lowered the papers to his lap and leaned his head against the headrest, shutting his eyes.

That wasn't a good idea, it turned out. All he saw was the hideous face and the words written in that desperate scrawl, "So I'm on the run, Mr. Lyons, and I don't know who to go to besides you."

Sorry, Danny.

Sorry you died so hard.

They say you're not completely dead and gone as long as there's a buddy who still remembers you. I remember you, so you're still around.

"No disrespect, Mr. Lyons, sir, but be real careful if you can help me I don't even know if you could take Lalo even though you are the Ironman."

Shit!

I can take him, Danny. And I will. For you. For me. For something bigger, something called justice and freedom, and a place where assholes like Lucero can't kill people who testify like the law tells them to do—can't put their heads in vises and squeeze the life right out their eye sockets.

I'll take him, Danny.

And I'll find out who Lucero has in the Justice Department, who it was that fingered you. And that's got to tie in to Judge Mayer somehow, because Brognola had me checking up on him, too. And if he's in-volved I'll take care of him, as well.

I'll take care of them all, Julie.

Damn, did I say "Julie"? I meant Danny. Julie, you bitch, how could you think I was lying to you? Well, to hell with you, anyway. I don't need you.

I'll take care of them all.

Just watch.

12

He fell asleep—really asleep—only one time during the flight. The nightmares were enough to keep him awake after that.

Hell, what was it all about, he wondered.

Moreover, why was it coming down on him all at once? He realized that he had been acting testy, as he admitted to Brognola on the telephone. The question was *why*.

Part of it was the lack of action.

Lyons knew that some men needed to face a physical challenge in order to feel alive. He knew that he was one of those men. A psychiatrist had explained it to him, once, a long time ago, when he paid a mandatory visit after his first shooting as a cop.

The same headshrinker had partially approved of Lyons's personal method of handling some of the stresses of the job, a method he had been a little embarrassed about up until then.

It all came about because his lieutenant on the LAPD had possessed some progressive ideas on mental health. Part of it was that even though the department didn't—at that time—require any officer involved in a shooting to visit a counselor, the lieutenant did.

So a cynical young Lyons had gone through the motions. And much to his surprise, he had found that the experience had a lot to commend itself.

The shrink he had drawn, named Dr. Hermann, was a youngish sort with a beard. Lyons wondered if you got bonus points on your psychiatry board examinations if you had a beard, especially if you had a name like Hermann. What was his first name, he wondered. Sigmund? Then he remembered that probably eighty percent of the cops wore mustaches, all so similar that a girl he had dated once referred to them as "standard, police-department-issue mustaches."

Well, this guy had a standard-issue shrink beard.

Aside from that, though, Dr. Hermann had a soft voice, soft comfortable chairs in his office and a particularly penetrating way of asking questions.

"How do you feel when you're going into a dangerous situation?" he had asked.

Lyons had been on the verge of making some smart-ass response, like it gave him a raging hard-on or something like that. He'd heard that concept suggested by others when talking about combat situations and, moreover, had read somewhere that such reactions were in fact common.

It was not the case with him, though. Besides, as long as he had to be there, Lyons figured he might as well try to get something out of it.

He thought about the question. "I don't really know. It's hard to say, actually. It's exciting, I guess. Especially if I don't know if I can take the guy or not."

"Why is it exciting? What is it about that experience that feels good?"

"The gamble, maybe. Like maybe I'll get my ass kicked or blown away."

"How do you feel afterward?"

"I feel alive. I feel alive during it, actually. But especially afterward. It makes me appreciate my life more. If I nearly got thumped but I won, then that feels good, too. To win. But even if it turns out not to have been a big risk, in hindsight, it still makes my life seem worth more, somehow."

The psychiatrist knew how to push the right buttons, Lyons had reflected. The short, simple questions got right to the point. They had made him look at things in a way he had never done before.

"Are you ever afraid?"

This was one Lyons had a ready, if ambiguous, answer for. "Yes and no," he responded promptly.

Dr. Hermann laughed. "You've been around the legal system too long already, Carl. That's a lawyer's answer."

Lyons interrupted before he could continue. "Whatever you do, don't call me a lawyer. Not ever. Men have died for less."

Not entirely sure if the Ironman meant it or not, the psychiatrist asked his next question. "What did you mean, 'yes and no'?"

Lyons composed his answer before speaking. "I'm not saying I'm a superhero or anything. Sure I'm afraid of being shot or getting hurt. I'm afraid of pain, just like the next guy."

"'If you cut us, do we not bleed,'" murmured Hermann to himself.

"What's that?"

"Oh, nothing. Sorry I interrupted you. Please continue."

"Well, like I said, I'm just as afraid as anybody else. So that's the 'yes' part. But I have a way of controlling it. Putting it out of my mind. And that's the 'no' part."

Dr. Hermann looked mildly interested, which for him was the height of emotional response. Lyons figured this reaction was roughly equal to a normal person jumping up and seizing him by the lapels, slamming him against the wall and screaming "Tell me! Tell me!"

"I turn off the TV."

The psychiatrist appeared to ponder this revelation. "And what does that mean?" he asked at last.

"Look," said Lyons, leaning forward from the comfortable chair and putting his forearms on his knees. "It's a gimmick, I admit. But it works for me, you know? So I do it."

"So tell me about it."

"I just visualize a TV. Just your regular, standard department-store-issue television set. And whatever I'm afraid of is showing on the screen." He hesitated. Somehow, saying it aloud made it sound silly, trivial.

"How do you do that?" Dr. Hermann's question was encouraging, reassuring.

"Sometimes it's a picture of a certain person or maybe a situation I'm afraid of. I actually visualize the bad guy on the screen. Or maybe I'll create a picture of me getting shot to shit, like it was a movie and I was watching it. Other times it's just the word, like 'fear' or 'pain' or 'death'."

"Go on."

Lyons noted that Dr. Hermann had folded his arms and was gazing almost intently at him. Shit, he thought, the guy must be beside himself with excitement.

"So I bring it up on the screen. And look at it. And then I just turn off the TV set."

"What does that do for you?"

"It helps me put it out of my mind. I imagine the image fading out, down to a pinpoint dot in the middle of the screen. Then it goes out entirely. And that means whatever I was afraid of is gone."

Dr. Hermann set down his pad and pencil and laced his hands behind his head. For several long moments he looked across the room, then a smile traced his lips.

"I like it," he said at last.

"What do you mean?"

"Here's what you may be doing when you do that," the doctor began. "First, by bringing it onto the screen, you are acknowledging your fear. That's an important step. And then you are putting it aside. That's what you do by turning off the TV set."

He thought for a moment, then nodded, almost to himself, and smiled again. "And as I think about it, there's an added benefit to making it an image on a TV screen."

"What's that?"

"I don't know if you intended this, I rather suppose you didn't. But a lot of forces that affect how we act are in many ways comparable to a television picture."

"How so?"

"Well, they aren't actually real, but they have a lot of qualities of reality about them. They seem real, in other words. And while you are looking at them, they might as well be real. But they can be controlled.''

He looked at Lyons and added, ''Which you are doing when you turn off the television set.''

The same psychiatrist had gone on to explain how some people needed an occasional challenge, even one that threatened their safety. He also suggested that this wasn't necessarily a bad thing. At least, it was acceptable unless the challenge became an obsession or unless it was for the wrong reasons.

Today, as Lyons gazed out the airplane window, he knew that part of the reason he had been ''testy'' was this restlessness, caused simply by a lack of action. But there was more than that.

The business with Julie was disturbing. It shouldn't bother him like that, he thought. Women are like buses, you miss one, another will come along pretty soon. Pay your fare, ride for a while, maybe transfer to another one.

But Julie was different.

He wondered what Dr. Hermann would have said to that.

Then that pitiful bastard, poor Danny Forbes, with his head in the vise; knowing about that hadn't helped his mood any.

His uneasiness had to do with the inhuman cruelty of the killing. Or maybe ''inhuman'' was the wrong term. Lyons couldn't imagine an animal doing that. But most of his problem stemmed from a vague, nonspecific guilt at not being able to help him.

The more he tried to make some sense of it, the less he could. Finally, he ''turned off the TV set,'' trying to put the whole mess out of his mind. Only temporarily, though, he told himself, so he could deal with it later.

Only this time turning off the TV set didn't do it.

So in his mind he unplugged it, then threw a blanket over it, as well. He even considered smashing the shit out of it but decided that was overreacting.

But he still didn't let himself go into a deep sleep. No more of those nightmares, thanks very much. Better to settle for a doze, something in which he could make sure nobody turned the set on.

Finally Lyons felt the jet make a subtle but noticeable downward shift in its path. That signified a decrease in altitude, and he realized Miami couldn't be too far away.

Actually, he reflected, "path" wasn't exactly the right word for it, but he couldn't come up with a more appropriate one.

"Trajectory" maybe would be better, like a bullet. Still, that made it sound like it was a natural or inevitable rise and fall, rather than one controlled—he hoped—by the pilot. Gadgets would probably say "vector," meaning a direction of force or some such bullshit scientific term.

To hell with it. "Path" worked fine for him.

The plane continued to descend. Lyons wondered why it always seemed that jet airliners did that by a gradual settling process, as if losing altitude by stages. Sink down some, then level out for a while. Why not just point the goddamn thing downward a little and go for it?

He supplied his own answer. It'd probably spill the drinks or something.

The "fasten seatbelts" sign came on; the pilot came over the loudspeaker and asked the stewardesses to seat themselves. Idly Lyons speculated whether they should be called "stewardi"—after all, it's not "octopusses," it's "octopi." Then he remembered that now, it couldn't be either "stewardesses" or "stewardi", it had to be "flight attendants," to avoid any sexist or other derogatory meaning.

Lyons had dated a few stewardesses, or stewardi, in his time. But, he'd never been out with a "flight attendant." Would it be any different? Would the new title make them more fun?

How much had it cost for all the bullshit necessary to make that change in airline terminology, he wondered sourly.

A ton of money, he'd be willing to bet. Attorneys telling them they had to do it, committees to recommend a new term, still other committees to approve what the first committees came up with, new forms that didn't use the old words, memos directed to "all personnel" explaining the new policies, and on and on.

Shit Ironman, he thought suddenly. What's with all the philosophical baloney? Are you getting old, or what?

In the seat next to him, Blancanales stretched his muscular frame. A pretty, dark-haired stewardess—flight attendant, that is—saw him and realized she had to attend to something in that area of the plane. As she passed them, her eyes met the Politician's.

"Can I get you anything, sir?"

Blancanales allowed his eyes to linger on her body for just a fraction of a second before he raised them to meet hers. It was just enough to be appreciative, not enough to be lewd.

"No. Thanks though."

"Will you be staying in Miami long?"

He winked. "Just a few days, probably. Just killing a little time here."

"Well, buzz me if you need anything."

"Thanks. I will." He watched her intently as she strolled, hips swaying, buttocks alternately tightening under the fabric of her flight attendant's outfit.

Next to him, Lyons shook his head. "I can't understand why she was so friendly to you," he said, "when I was so close by and available."

"Animal magnetism, Ironman."

"Animal magnetism, my ass." Lyons lapsed into a moody silence and stared out the window.

"What's on your mind, Homes?" the Politician inquired. "Your 'alleged mind,' that is," he added.

Lyons shook his head. "Ahh, nothing," he said disgustedly. "Bunch of different bullshit, that's all."

"Somethin' eating at you, buddy?" The Politician's face showed his concern.

Lyons continued to gaze out the window for several moments. There seemed to be no way to explain it in less than an hour. So he gave the short form.

"Man, I don't know what it is. I just feel sluggish. Like I want to be doing something, but I don't know what. That plus a sort of 'what the fuck' attitude, if you know what I mean."

Blancanales nodded. "I know exactly what you mean. I get it sometimes. Feel restless, without knowing why. Sort of a nonspecific anger, too. Maybe a little depressed."

"What do you mean, 'nonspecific anger'?"

"Like I'm pissed off at the world in general, but I don't know what caused it or why. Like I want to find somebody to blame for it but I can't."

Lyons looked at his friend. It never ceased to amaze him how insightful the guy was.

"That's it. I think maybe it started when I saw the pictures of that pitiful bastard in the vise. When it's somebody you know..." He didn't finish the sentence.

"Yeah. Makes it more personal, even if it wasn't some kind of close friend who died. Just brings it closer to home, somehow. Plus it emphasizes the finality of everything."

"What do you mean?" inquired Lyons.

"Well, death is pretty permanent, and..."

"So tell me something I don't know," Lyons interrupted. The tone of his voice clearly emphasized how irritated he was.

"What I'm trying to say is that it means you can't ever go back. Gadgets says that when somebody you know dies, it just reinforces the fact that time keeps on going. Makes you realize that what once was can never be again."

A couple of long minutes passed. Lyons still didn't reply. Finally, as the plane banked into its final approach to the airport, Blancanales took up the thread again. "Of course, there is one cure."

"Cure for what?"

"For those nonspecific blues you're talking about."

"What's that?"

Seeing the quizzical look on his partner's face, Blancanales went on, a faint smile tugging at the corners of his mouth. "Get yourself in the middle of a shit-storm of a firefight. Cures it every time."

Lyons's face slowly spread into a grin. "I guess it would, at that. Hard to worry about this heavy philosophical crap when you're trying to keep your ass from getting shot off."

"Takes your mind off of it, amigo. Rearranges your priorities, so to speak."

After a moment Lyons's smile grew even broader. "Plus, you get to kill some assholes. There's nothing like being able to shoot the hell out of something to make you feel better. Especially if it's bad guys. It works every time."

The Politician returned the grin. "Welcome back to the world, amigo. I was beginning to worry about you."

"No sweat, partner."

"Well, it's not like you, all the cerebral bullshit, this Hamlet at Elsinore bit. But if you can still get excited about blowing away people, you're okay."

"Like we used to say in football practice," Lyons observed, " 'blood makes the grass grow.' "

"What about Astroturf?"

Lyons didn't answer. The plane bumped onto the runway, then began its ground journey to the air terminal.

13

For some reason the jet didn't actually approach the terminal at Miami International Airport. Instead, a staircase was driven out to the plane, and the passengers were asked to depart that way.

The tropical night air enveloped the two men as they walked the sixty-odd yards to the terminal.

Strangely, the moment he stepped off the plane Lyons felt his spirits do a complete reversal, a mood one-eighty. His earlier lethargy vanished as he felt the heavy, warm air.

As they walked across the tarmac Lyons looked around to orient himself. He figured out which direction was north, then looked off into the darkness and the distant lights.

North of the airport would be Hialeah. That's where the racetrack was, he recalled. It was a largely Hispanic area, and it was bordered on the east by Liberty City. When the bloody riots shook Miami in 1980, they had been in and around Liberty City.

Almost due east of the airport was Miami proper. Beyond that, still farther east, across Biscayne Bay, would be the city of Miami Beach. It was located on a peninsula—hell, it *was* the peninsula—that hung down into the ocean.

It had always helped Lyons to visualize things. Somebody once described Miami Beach by telling him to take his left hand and hold it up in front of his face, palm facing him. Put the fingers together, but the hand stays open, not curled into a fist. Then separate the thumb, so it goes up a half inch or so from the side of the hand.

Now turn the hand upside down. Make it so the fingertips point downward, but the palm is still toward the face. It's awkward, of course. The thumb now hangs down to the right of the hand.

The fingers and the palm of the hand are the southern portion of Florida. Miami Beach is the thumb. The space between the palm and the thumb is Biscayne Bay.

Lyons smiled as he recalled it. The woman who had given him this description was an artist, used to thinking in images. For a fleeting moment he wondered if she was still alive. And, if so, what she was doing these days.

Once, years ago, Lyons had spent a couple of weeks in the Miami area. It had been part business and part pleasure, and he had loved it. The business part had been a mission. The pleasure part had been a friend, the artist.

This time, between what had been done to Danny Forbes and his fight with Julie, it would be all business, he thought grimly.

He remembered Little Havana, just west of downtown Miami, with its large Cuban population, its strong black coffee and fine handmade cigars.

Lalo would have ties in Little Havana, he thought grimly. He would probably not live there—as a big-shot gangster he would be above that—but his roots would be there.

Three bridges ran from Miami to Miami Beach, Tuttle Causeway at the top, Venetian Causeway in the middle and MacArthur Causeway at the bottom.

He recalled that as you went east from Little Havana, through old Miami and its downtown district, you would come to Biscayne Bay. The MacArthur Causeway would dump you into the southern tip of Miami Beach, namely Ocean Drive and Collins Avenue.

This was the center of the art deco hotels, most of them built in the thirties and forties.

Though he didn't fancy himself much of a connoisseur of the different styles of either decor or architecture, Lyons liked the art deco area. To him it was both old-fashioned and modern, the funky blend—or clash—of strong lines, chrome, etched glass and offbeat windows.

And everywhere, seemingly everywhere at least, the palm trees jutted like spires into the skyline.

Lyons felt his pulse quicken. The tropics always brought on that special sensation, he reflected.

He glanced at Blancanales. His friend and partner wore the same look of expectancy on his face. The Politician turned and winked at him.

"Getting fired up, Homes?"

Lyons nodded. "You?" he inquired.

"*Sí*, amigo."

At midday it would be so hot it would seem as if the heat were pressing down on you, Lyons reflected. But now, at night, the warmth held a certain tension, a sort of electricity to it. Lyons inevitably got the feeling that beneath the veneer of civilization, the supermarkets and shopping centers, violence was always close at hand.

Violence and death.

The humid night air seemed tangible. It was almost as if it had a substance and an ardor of its own. It charged him with energy. Before he had felt a restless inaction. Now that was gone, and in its place was a restless—and reckless—thirst *for* action.

He wondered if it was the Latin influence that created the feeling. A barely disguised brutality seemed just around the corner on nights like this.

This very evening men and women would kill other men and women. Hell, chances were it was happening even as they crossed the tarmac to the terminal.

There would be bar fights. They began as arguments and ended as deadly assaults, where alcohol added fuel to the night's inherent energy.

Somebody would make a lewd comment about somebody else's woman. Pushing would lead to blows. Then the weapons, the knives and guns, would come out. A thrust, a quick slice or the explosion of gunfire. The grunt of surprise and shock from the man whose body felt the blade or bullet.

Blood would flow, as warm and wet as the night air itself.

Elsewhere, somebody would make a crack about the Tampa Bay Buccaneers being bush league compared to the Dolphins. Or that the USFL was worse than college ball. Fists would fly, bottles would be grabbed and broken against the rail of pool tables, teeth would be knocked out by cues.

And then there would be the eternal triangles.

Women would catch their men with other women. Men would do ditto. Emotions would go from zero to out of control and more people would die. Lyons tried to remember the legal term for it. It was something invented by a judge in medieval England, yet it was used even today.

Then he had it. "Heat of passion."

The phrase meant the sudden, extreme emotional anger that exploded in a person who caught a loved one in the act with somebody else.

Even if he lost his cool, went berserk and killed the other guy or his old lady—as Lyons's instructor at the police academy had put it—or both, the law made it manslaughter instead of murder. Why? Because the killing occurred in the "heat of passion."

Countless sexual unions would be occurring that night, as well.

Some would be for fun, some for love, some for money. Couples would couple in cars, in deserted areas, in houses and apartments, on balconies. Sweat would coat their bodies and mingle as the tension increased in a gasping, spasmodic oh, baby, oh, baby, or yes, oh, yes, oh, ye-e-e-sss . . .

Drugs woud be dealt in the hot summer night.

On the streets and in the nightclubs, it would be consumer level. Men would meet and deal, a nervous exchange of currency for a small folded paper bindle of powder. At higher levels, thick bundles of bills would be traded for kidney-sized plastic bags of powder, by men with eyes as cold and deadly as frozen steel.

Lyons wondered what it would be like to be a cop here.

Like L.A. in the summertime, there would be no lack of action. Young men and women, some of them just twenty-one or twenty-two years old, trying to keep the lid on the raw emotions of life and death, love and hate, lust and hurt.

Hot blood, he thought.

The tropics made for hot blood. Death in the afternoon, passion in the night. It drove men into a hyperactive gamble of lives and emotions, playing at the big tables. And all the while, a feeling of violent death waited to explode.

Blood could be spilled on Spanish tile in the morning, and a wedding take place on the same spot only hours later. It was easy to understand why bullfighting had originated in places with climates like this.

The lure of death. The lure of money, the big score.

The big tables, Lyons reflected. The lure was there. High stakes. Big money. The dealer hits on sixteen, stands on seventeen. What does he do on eighteen and nineteen? Kill?

And, on top of it all was the White Madame, the Snow Princess, Lady 'Caine.

Narcotics had brought a new dimension to the tropical violence Lyons always sensed. The cocaine trade made its impact on the city in much the same way as the drug itself affected the individual user—a brittle glamour, a false confidence, an artificial drive.

Downhill.

Destination, the pits.

Of course, it didn't feel like that at the time. A roller coaster was an accurate metaphor—climbing higher, dizzying forces on the turns, joyous screams of laughter. But up close it was different. Each shrieking downward surge ended up a little lower than the last one. The laughs became tinged with desperation; what started out as a frolic became frenetic.

The shining silver of mirrors. The sharp precision of razor blades chopping up and down to make powder from the chunks. The nervous laughter of the new user, the deadly intensity of the addicted pro.

Another fast rush to nowhere.

The profits, Lyons knew, were incredible, virtually beyond comprehension.

A single good-sized coke deal traded a suitcase filled with plastic bags of white power for a suitcase filled with more money than a corporate vice-president made in two years. And that didn't even take into account the big importers, getting the stuff into the United States in the first place.

Lyons remembered the photographs Grogan had showed him, hideous pictures of a man with his head in a vise. What could make one man do that to another?

That kind of money would do it.

It twisted the mind. It warped reality. It pulled with a force that would corrupt all but the strongest. And when it was added to the glittery lure of the drug itself, the forces became stacked one on top of the other and the seduction would be all but irresistible.

As with every wild party, though, there would be some breakage.

Human breakage.

The party would move on to another location. It would keep going, as though it had a life of its own. In its wake would be strewn the broken lives, the shattered emotions, the despoiled souls, the careers and lives and loves gone, sacrificed to the call of the Snow Siren.

"Coke isn't addictive."

"Hey, man, I can handle it."

"It's okay as long as I control myself."

And, "Hey, honey, you just gotta be a party lady. It's not hooking. Nobody's paying you for it. You're gonna be putting out because you're havin' a good time. It'll be a great party, lotta lights, big swimming pool—course you don't need a swimsuit—all the C you want. Just make sure you look good."

Coke whores, they used to call it on the strike force. If they were pretty or had big tits, the C was on the house.

And the insidious but inevitable move to dealing.

"I'm not a *real* dealer," they used to say. "I only supply my friends. Just enough for their own use."

"Isn't that dealing?" Lyons would ask.

"Well, they'd get it somewhere, anyway."

"So?"

"So they might as well get it from me. They can trust me. Besides, it helps me pay for my own."

And that, Lyons knew, was the real reason users became dealers. Hell, the shit's expensive. Even if the guy's pulling down forty grand a year, it's easy, real easy, hell, ridiculously easy, to do a hundred a week. That's beginner stuff, party quantities.

So knock four hundred a month net off his income. See how that affects his standard of living. Especially considering how short the high is.

So next time he buys a little more than he needs and sells off the rest. "Just to his friends," of course. Make enough profit on that so it pays for his own.

Why, shit, his own was free, that way. And the guy's still got his job, so he's not going to deal to *make money*, no sir-ee, just to pay for his own.

And then they start thinking. There's probably nothing wrong with making just a *little* money off it....

Lyons had heard all the excuses. He had seen all the lies. First as a cop, then on the strike force, he had seen the aftermath of the party. And he had known what it all added up to.

Bullshit. Self-delusion. Self-destruction. The superhighway to nowhere.

Yeah, this would be the perfect finishing school for an animal like Lalo.

Lyons knew that the Cuban killer must have stood there in that National City warehouse, smoking his brown cigarettes and giving instructions.

"More," he might have said. Or maybe it would have been in Spanish, *"Mas."*

And somebody else would have turned the massive worm drive a quarter turn, moving the jaws fractionally closer together. The skull would be resilient at first, like a green branch. The point would be reached, however, where...

The Miami Crush.

The crush of power. The crush of drugs. The crushing of emotions by the cocaine lure. The crushing of lives by those who imported it.

The crushing of skulls by their enforcers.

Back in the detective bureau of National City Police, Lyons had decided that Lalo must have enjoyed watching the torture. Now, as he felt again the power of the coke kingdom, he wasn't so sure.

The Ironman knew that a lot of torturers got a sick pleasure out of the infliction of pain on their victims. And he originally put Lalo in that category—a pro, sure, but also somebody who liked what he was doing.

That was an attractive theory. It worried him that it might not be true.

First, it somehow made the evil easier to handle to say that this was the work of a single, twisted mind. To say otherwise was to admit that lust and greed could create an endless supply of Lalo's.

Moreover, if Lalo got a personal sick gratification from what he did, it gave him a weakness. That weakness would make him vulnerable. It was something that Able Team could perhaps exploit. But if he just did it for business—part of the game—that weakness wouldn't be there.

Maybe he was just a purely evil son of a bitch. Maybe that was all there was to it.

"Bad magic," according to the word on the streets and Danny's letter, the one that had become his last will and testament.

It would be all pro, all the way. It would mean major leagues, heavy hitters for sure.

This is what we do to informants. If you're not for us, you're against us. Lady 'Caine was a jealous bitch indeed, and her friends were even worse.

As he and Blancanales entered the air terminal Lyons predicted that Lalo would be there, somewhere, he and his army of killers. They were a necessary part of the cocaine empire. Miami was the perfect environment for a man like that.

It was also a fitting place for him to die.

Carl Lyons did not consider himself possessed of any particular psychic or extrasensory abilities, yet he felt one thing with certainty. And he felt it although they didn't even have their orders, officially. Hell, they hadn't even been informed of the mission. Officially.

Still, he knew what lay ahead.

Lalo and Able Team were on a collision course.

They—Lyons, Blancanales, and Gadgets—would find the Cuban killer and his men. And when they did, blood would spill, wherever it happened to be.

It might be in some modern high rise, all glass and mirrors and plush. In that case, crimson blood would splash on expensive walls. It would run in little rivulets down glass-and-chrome furnishings to be soaked up by thick carpeting.

Or it might take place in some tenement, made of tan or white or pink stucco perhaps, with clotheslines strung behind them. There would be blood-red spatters on the rough surfaces of the walls, and red stains turning to brown on the dirty pavement of some black alley.

But when it was over, either Able Team or Lalo and his army of killers would be dead.

Bad magic versus the good guys; one side had to die.

14

Inside the terminal the public address system squawked its barely recognizable announcement.

"Will Delta Airlines passenger Mr. Charles Leanord please pick up a white courtesy telephone?"

From long practice in undercover roles, Lyons rarely had any difficulty remembering who he was supposed to be. He veered off from the Politician and found one of the telephones.

He identified himself and the operator said, "Just one moment, sir, there's a party on hold for you. I'll connect you."

Brognola, thought Lyons, shaking his head in mild amusement. He's figured out we advanced our flight. Hell, good as the Bear is, he probably reprogrammed the airline's computers so they had to notify him to approve the change in Mr. Leanord's and Mr. Balcazar's reservations.

Well, the chief doesn't miss a trick, that's for sure. He won't care, of course, but he's calling just to remind us that he knows everything we do.

The telephone clicked in his ear and then the connection was made, and Lyons could sense that the party was on the other end of the line. "Yeah, Chief," he said.

"Thanks for the promotion, buddy," came the cheerful, friendly voice of Gadgets Schwarz.

"Gadgets!"

Lyons barked the name of his friend into the telephone.

Any traces of his earlier depression had vanished, for the time being, anyway. His anguish over the business with Julie was sure to crop up again, he knew. For now, however, even that had given way to the exhilaration of being with his partners, doing what they did best.

All the ingredients were there. A strange city. A mission. A chance to balance the books a little. Hell, a chance to do some good in a world where there wasn't a lot of that being done. Or so it sometimes seemed, anyway. It gave him a sense of purpose, heightened by the danger.

Blancanales had been right on the money. Nothing like the prospect of getting your ass shot off to take your mind off your other problems.

Besides, he thought, I'll win either way. At least, each way has something going for it, he amended hastily. Whether I really win or not is debatable.

One way, I get in a big firefight and I survive it. If that happens, that's good. I will have done some good and lived through it. Then either I can patch things up with her, or I can't. And even if I can't, a successful mission will make me feel better.

The other way, I get in a big firefight and I *don't* survive it. And if that happens, Lyons thought, then at least I don't have to worry about that other bullshit anymore.

In a way, it was a sort of freedom. You win a little no matter how it goes.

He spoke into the telephone. "Gadgets, buddy, where the hell are you? What are you doing here, already?"

"I'm supposed to be meeting you there at the airport," came the reply.

"Then why the hell aren't you here?" demanded Lyons in a phony anger.

"I got delayed a little."

Then it struck Lyons that Brognola and Kurtzman must have been checking up on them, after all. "How'd you know our flight, anyway?"

"The Bear. I guess you guys had some later flight, but the Bear had it rigged so if that reservation was changed, they'd be notified. So they told me your ETA when I checked in with them."

"So what held you up anyway?"

"It's a long story. I'll tell you later. When I see you," he added.

"When'll that be?"

"Ohh—" Gadgets stretched the word out, and Lyons imagined his partner was consulting his watch and making some rapid calculations "—give me an hour."

"An hour!"

"It could be that long. I gotta line up a car." Then he paused. "Look, if you don't feel like hanging around the airport that long, why don't you guys rent the car and come to where I am?"

"Where's that? No, wait a minute, I gotta get something to write on."

Lyons hunched up one shoulder to hold the telephone against his ear, while he pulled a pen from his shirt pocket. Then he patted his pockets, looking for something to write on. Finally he found his boarding pass.

"Shoot," he said when he was ready.

Gadgets gave him the directions to the Marriott Hotel on Biscayne Bay.

Lyons let out a low whistle. "You're high rolling it for sure, aren't you, buddy? Now I see why you're not here. You're too busy scoping out the scenery there." Even as late as it was, Lyons figured things would be pretty active in that part of town.

"Nah, not really. Actually I just had car trouble, that's all. See you when you get here," said Gadgets.

"Ten-fourskin," replied Lyons.

SOME, TEN MILES from the airport, Gadgets hung up the telephone.

He was in the room he had rented for them in the luxurious new Marriott. Lyons was right. This was a little ritzier than they were used to. Brognola was not exactly a tightwad where his men were concerned. Still, he did not make a habit of putting them up in superdeluxe resort hotels complete with their own marinas.

"Hell, if you get in a brawl there and start breaking stuff, it costs too much to replace," he once explained genially. "Let alone if it's some big goddamn firefight."

What do you mean, one of them—Lyons, if Gadgets's memory served him well—had demanded.

''Hell, somebody with an Uzi on autoburn inside the bar of one of those fancy joints could destroy fifty thousand dollars in booze just with one sweep. I can't afford to replace that.''

Well, thought Gadgets, today was different. The chief would just have to lump it this time.

Gadgets was probably not afraid of much of anything in the world. He'd been tortured, but he'd come through with his brain and nerve cells more or less intact. He'd seen a lot of death. And, like the others on the Stony Man enterprise, he'd engineered a good bit of it himself.

Today, though, he'd come as close as he'd ever been to the grim reaper. The bony old chap with the scythe had taken a hell of a good run at him, and Gadgets had barely dodged the sweep of the blade.

The experience had left him decidedly jumpy.

It left him so jumpy that when the Marriott had loomed up before him, it had just *felt* like a safe place to hole up. Gadgets hadn't hesitated a second.

And, even now, though the effects of the episode were gone, the idea of sitting in the room and waiting for his partners didn't hold much appeal for him. It didn't matter that the room was the most luxurious one he'd been in for quite a while. The hunted animal in him wanted to be somewhere besides a cave with no back door.

The bar would do it. Room to run, cover to hide.

In his mid-thirties, Hermann ''Gadgets'' Schwarz stood five-ten and weighed in at one-seventy. He had a square-shaped face and a strong, solid jaw, but no one feature caught the eye.

He regarded this as an asset.

One pair of contact lenses and three pairs of glasses—the glasses each with different frames—were all he needed for several disguises. All but the most trained observer would see four different people, depending on which frames he had on.

Wire frames made him look like a scholar from an East Coast university, the kind of guy who specialized in medieval English history, perhaps.

Steel frames let him pass for anything from an accountant to a computer programmer to a Porsche mechanic. In fact, he had successfully impersonated each in the past. The performances in each case had been enhanced by the fact that he was well qualified to do all three roles.

Heavy black frames and a dark suit made him a banker or possibly a director of some major corporation. The effect was complete when he announced himself in an imperiously gruff voice as "Herr Schwarz, ze shairman of ze board."

When he was really being "just Gadgets," he was the third member of Able Team, a genius-level electronics and computer whiz. And, no matter which disguise he employed on a particular occasion, he was—like Lyons and Blancanales—one of the most skilled killers in the world.

He was also an incurable practical joker.

One time, while attending an electronics school right after high school, Gadgets and some of his friends had been at pizza house. A crowd of "frat rats," hot-shit Ivy League students from a fraternity at a nearby exclusive private college, had occupied the adjoining table.

The rumpled electronics tinkerers had become the target of verbal abuse from the silver-spoon types in their little letterman's jackets and tennis togs.

Gadgets and his comrades ignored it for a while. Finally, the silver-spooners—fortified with liquid courage and the knowledge that they outnumbered the gadgeteers—began to get physical about it.

The electronics types finally picked up and left. This was before Vietnam and before hours of specialized training in the ways to kill that he would later receive, both officially from Uncle Sam and unofficially from Mack Bolan. And though it was clearly the right thing to do, Gadgets and his friends did not like to think of themselves as backing off from a fight.

What the Ivy Leaguers could not have known, however, was that it was not nice to fuck with Gadgets, even then. In fact, it was a big mistake.

The revenge wasn't immediate. But when it came, there was no denying who had won.

The young Schwarz undertook a campaign of sorts. First he located the fraternity house. Then he reconned it, posing as a telephone repairman.

The telephone repairman had to use the bathroom. He was in there a long time, but nobody paid any particular attention. After all, "he was only a workman."

Nobody noticed that he had taken his toolbox inside with him.

That night happened to be the fraternity-sorority ball, a formal event held at the frat house.

It would begin at eight.

Also, on that night the first person who happened to sit on the toilet seat after eight o'clock was going to receive a special surprise about fifteen seconds after he or she sat down. The surprise was an electrical nip of about five thousand volts.

The charge was delivered at a very low amperage, or current, of course. Gadgets had carefully designed it to avoid actually electrocuting anybody. That would, he realized, be a little extreme, even for the abuse they had taken at the pizza joint.

It was a sophisticated device. The young Schwarz had actually built a timer into it, so that it didn't become operational until that evening. And it was so cleverly concealed that it went undetected until the first person received the jolt.

He couldn't have planned it better.

The recipient of the voltage was none other than the dean's wife. An imperious woman in her late fifties, she and her husband had put in a courtesy appearance at the party. Nature had called about the time the electrical device went on line.

The dean's wife was not amused. Her shriek of outrage—a scream, actually—was heard throughout the frat house.

The dean was even less amused.

He shut down the party, suspended the fraternity and ordered the president and the other officers to report to his office at nine o'clock the following Monday morning. When they went out to their cars shortly before eight-thirty that morning, a neat, computer-printed note greeted them.

> If it happened once, it could happen again. Beware.
>
> Signed,
> Anchovy's Raiders

This particular evening, however, Gadgets was not in a mood for joking. His own words, written so many years before, applied to him as well. "If it happened once, it could happen again...."

His back still hurt, but not too badly. Best way to look at all this, Hermann, he told himself, is that now we know. It's open season, and there's no bag limit.

After he got off the phone with Lyons, he tucked a Kissinger-modified .45 Government Model in his waistband and put a light jacket over it. He put two spare clips in the jacket, then checked the mirror to make sure his armaments weren't too obvious. That done, he took the elevator down to the bar. He found a dark corner, near a back door, ordered a gin and tonic and settled down to wait.

The orders had reached him earlier that day, direct from Stony Man Farm.

Go directly to Miami.

Do not pass go. Do not collect two hundred dollars. When you get there, go to the convention center in downtown Miami.

At a certain location will be a certain blue Dodge van, courtesy of the Feds with whom you will be working, the orders went. It'll have all your usual equipment, mainly weaponry, inside it.

The ignition key will be tucked under the front wheel on the driver's side.

It was a standard routine, one they had used before, and Gadgets knew it well. You go up, holding your keys to unlock the door, then drop your keys "accidentally," and when you bend to pick them up, you come up with the van key, as well.

Go to a motel—not the Marriott—and check in, then call the Farm for further instructions.

Gadgets started to do as he was told. He had arrived in Miami a couple of hours earlier and had caught a cab to the convention center. The cab departed and he walked to the van, taking out his keys as he did so, then apparently dropping them.

As he stooped to recover both sets of keys, something caught his eyes beneath the driver's door. It was illuminated by the parking lot lights.

It was red. And small, less than an inch long. It was about as big around as a piece of dried spaghetti.

The electronics man in him came to full alert.

Insulation. It was the rubbery plastic stuff that went around the outside of a piece of wire. What you strip off the wire when you need to get to the bare metal to make a connection.

Now, what in the world would a piece of insulation be doing under the van?

Car stereos use wire like that, he thought. Radios, amplifiers, tape players—sound systems of all types. The vehicle itself uses wire like that. Hell, half the van's own wiring probably used that kind of wire. Practical jokes, like shocking devices wired into toilet seats to give somebody a surprise, could use wire like that.

And while we're talking surprises, why, golly, gee whiz, bombs usually involve such wires, Gadgets thought.

Wouldn't it be funny if somebody accidentally left a bomb in the van they had conveniently arranged for Able Team to pick up?

His mind performed lightning-fast calculations.

If it was a bomb, chances are it was wired to the ignition—otherwise, no reason for a piece of insulation to be there. If it was wired to the ignition, it wouldn't go off until he started the engine. That meant he would be safe opening the door.

Sometimes, though, people who used such bombs controlled them by a radio signal.

That made it foolproof. Somebody could be sitting across the parking lot, watching him. That person would be waiting with his, or her, finger on a button. When the button was pushed, it would make his own fraternity gag seem like child's play.

Key poised at the lock in the van's door, Gadgets glanced casually around the lot.

The van had been parked at the far end of the lot. The other cars were closer to the buildings. Nothing looked suspicious, nothing looked out of place as he scanned the asphalt plane with its white marks designating the parking spaces.

Then a single vehicle came into sharp focus.

Maybe it was some sixth sense; Gadgets had experienced that before. Maybe the attention that was concentrated on Gadgets by the people inside the car somehow transmitted itself to him.

It was a Ferrari.

Black. Long, low, sleek, an aerodynamic missile of a car, parked across the lot. Even as he glanced around, trying to look casual, he could see the dark forms of somebody inside it.

Gadgets didn't hesitate an instant. Better to act and look foolish if you're wrong, than to not act and look dead.

He sprinted away from the van. His sturdy legs churned the asphalt lot beneath his feet. At the last instant, heedless of the skin on his elbows and forearms, he launched himself into a low, flat, headfirst dive, like a swimmer in a race going off the blocks into the pool.

Gadgets fancied he could feel the finger push the button from inside the Ferrari.

The van exploded with a tremendous blast that shook the ground.

The shock wave helped propel the diving Able Team member forward. A brilliant orange petrochemical ball erupted into the night sky. It was accompanied by pieces of the van's body. Even in the midst of the explosion, Gadgets's computerlike brain somehow saw and registered that one of the doors had been blasted in his direction.

It missed him and landed with a heavy metallic crash some eight feet away.

Later Gadgets figured that he had actually heard two blasts, so close together as to be virtually indistinguishable. The first was undoubtedly the bomb itself; the second, the gasoline and ammunition in the van.

In the aftermath of the detonation, pieces of steel and glass rained down on the lot. The burning roared in his ears as Gadgets, half-stunned, tried to crawl away from the fireball.

Another sound reached his ears.

It was the throaty growl of an expensive race car engine. The screech of tires on asphalt followed immediately.

Gadgets twisted on the pavement, trying to retrieve the .45 from his belt as the sleek shape of the Ferrari bore down on him.

15

Still dazed from the explosion, Gadgets saw the Ferrari roaring straight toward him.

The race car's acceleration was phenomenal. It seemed to grab the pavement and leap ahead, jerking the asphalt under its wheels. At first it swerved in a mild fishtail. Then it straightened out and bore down on him.

From the front it resembled a sleek black shark on wheels.

Pieces of the van were still falling from the sky as Gadgets struggled to gain control of his body from the shock. Slowly, his coordination returned. He could almost see it occur and feel his nerves shake off the shock of the concussion. But even then he knew the .45 was not the answer.

Oh, he could probably get to it in time. That wasn't the problem.

And he could even manage to get off a couple of shots, most likely. And if he were real lucky he'd nail the driver, assuming the heavy silver-tip slugs didn't ricochet off the sharply slanting windscreen.

Of course, the latter point was a big assumption, a major "if."

Gadgets knew there were some things a .45 does well. However, penetrating the safety-glass windshield of an onrushing Ferrari wasn't one of them.

Not that it was the weapon's fault. Gadgets knew that. The gun had been designed for a specific purpose, to be a man stopper. Well, it was that, all right. In spades. Like, if a bullet hit a guy it would knock his ass to the ground and then stomp on him a little. That's what they had asked of the .45 and that's what it did. If the job required something else, design another weapon.

But Gadgets knew that even if he got really lucky, what did it get him? Unless the dying driver jerked the wheel, the driverless missile would still be aimed at him.

The thought of the front and rear wheels rolling over the body of Leo and Helen Schwarz's son, Hermann, did not thrill him.

Forcing reluctant muscles to respond, he ignored the gun and pushed himself to his feet.

Engine making a finely tuned roar, the Ferrari bore down on him.

Fear charged him with adrenaline, like Popeye responding to his spinach. He crouched. The gap closed. At the last instant he leaped straight upward into the air. He tucked his legs upward as he jumped, curling his body around them. His body slowly rotated until his back was parallel to the ground, like an Olympic high jumper clearing the bar.

He almost made it.

The top edge of the windshield hit him as he hung in the air for that microsecond of time, in which upward motion had stopped but downward motion hadn't yet begun.

"Aaaghhh!"

The sound exploded from his throat under the impact.

Fortunately, most of his body was above the vector of force of the onrushing car. It hit him a glancing blow and spun his body around like a top. He rolled over and on top of the race car, then fell to the ground behind it.

Smoke rose from the tires as the Ferrari screeched to a halt, sliding around as it slewed and slowed.

Once is enough, thought Gadgets.

He had landed heavily on his side. Still charged with adrenaline, he scrambled into a sitting position, the .45 now in his hand. The Ferrari had slid to a stop broadside to him, the passenger side toward him, some thirty yards away.

It all seemed to happen in slow motion.

The door started to open. A figure started to get out. A man. And, in the man's hand, a gun.

In the distance a siren wailed.

The man with the gun stepped out of the car. His intentions weren't hard to guess, and they didn't seem friendly. Probably wants to finish the job, thought Gadgets.

Gadgets carried his .45 "cocked and locked." That meant it was ready for action—one in the chamber, hammer cocked—except that the notch-style safety was in place.

The .45 was in his hands. Cocked and locked became cocked and unlocked. The blunt steel sights steadied on the target by the Ferrari. Gadgets aimed carefully, gripping the weapon in both hands. He was sitting on the ground, feet flat in front of him, knees up, elbows on his knees to steady the man stopper.

Boom! Boom! Boom!

The pistol jumped in his hand after each shot, the slide opening and slamming shut each time.

Three in the ten-ring, he thought.

The man was slammed back into the open doorway of the Ferrari as though hit with a baseball bat swung by a major league heavy-hitter. In terms of the energy transmitted by the slugs, that was probably accurate. He staggered backward, falling against the car.

With a screech of tires the car leaped ahead. It disappeared into the night, a black shadow streaking across the parking lot. The gunman's body was dragged, half in and half out of the open door, for a few yards. Then it came free and rolled to a lumpy stop.

Gadgets thought about putting another one or two into the still form, just for drill.

No time.

The sound of sirens intensified, drawing closer. Stiffly Gadgets forced himself to his feet.

This was not the time to be a good citizen and hang around to give a report to the police. He soon found that his legs worked all right, and he loped into the darkness, out of the lot, away from the petroleum bonfire that had been the van.

One thing was sure, he thought.

The opening gambit had definitely been made.

16

Gadgets finished recounting the tale to his two companions.

The three Stony Man warriors were in their room in the Marriott Hotel. Lyons and Blancanales had arrived some half an hour after Gadgets's call to the airport. They had bought a bottle of Johnny Walker Black Label and adjourned upstairs, where Gadgets brought them up to date.

"You okay, amigo?" Blancanales inquired of Gadgets.

Gadgets nodded. "I lost some skin off my elbows, and a few of my ribs are a little sore. But otherwise, everything's okay."

"Ears ringing?"

"Negative. Not anymore, anyway."

After a moment Lyons turned their attention to the tactical implications of the incident. "Did you get a chance to check out the guy you shot?"

Gadgets shrugged. "Not really. I looked him over as I ran by. Dark complexion. In his twenties. Had a MAC-10, it looked like."

"Cuban?" inquired Blancanales.

"Looked like it."

Lyons, trained investigator that he was, pleaded the subject one more time. "Anything else at all that you recall about the guy?"

Their partner wrinkled his brow as if deep in thought. Then his face brightened. "Come to think of it, there was."

"What?" asked Lyons excitedly.

"He had some unusual markings on him."

"Tattoos?"

"Not exactly."

"Well, what kind of markings, then? Scars?"

"They looked like holes, actually. Three of them. In his chest. I got the impression he hadn't had them for very long."

Blancanales leaned back and laughed out loud. "Great. What an observer! We'll be able to recognize that guy if we ever run into him again!"

Turning to Gadgets, the Politician suddenly looked serious. "Three of them, you say?"

Gadgets nodded.

"Kinda round?"

"Yeah."

"Each one about . . . oh, say forty-five-hundredths of an inch in diameter? Give or take five-thousandths either way." Blancanales was specifying the size of a .45-caliber slug in his questions.

Gadgets pretended to be amazed. "Almost exactly!" he said excitedly. "That's amazing! How'd you know?"

Blancanales shrugged in feigned modesty. "It was nothing, really. Just a lucky guess, is all."

Lyons stared at them, then simply shook his head. "Well, I guess you're okay, anyway," he said finally.

The tension broken, Lyons went back to business.

"So, what did Brognola say?"

"A lot."

"So, tell us."

Gadgets took a deep breath, then recounted his discussion with the Stony Man chief.

It had been a long conversation.

They had looked into the possibility that there was a leak in the Justice Department, Brognola had informed him. It would be somebody owned by Lucero, as the desperate letter from Danny Forbes had indicated.

They had it narrowed down. The prime suspect was a narcotics agent in the DEA.

Lyons looked grim as Gadgets recounted this bit of information. "An agent, eh?" he inquired.

Gadgets nodded.

It was no secret among them that to Lyons a dirty cop was as bad as a traitor to the country. It was a violation of duty to the job. Moreover, it stood for a betrayal of fellow officers, who were sacrificing their own sleep and marriages and sometimes lives to make a case.

"Who was he?" Lyons said at last.

Gadgets continued his account of Brognola's briefing.

The leak was a senior guy on one of the Drug Task Force Teams. He had a lot of access to sensitive cases brought by the federal prosecutors in Miami.

The van incident pretty much cinched it.

"At least something good came out of that," Gadgets editorialized with a good-natured grin.

It seemed that Kurtzman, acting on Brognola's instructions, had arranged for the van. It was to be equipped and made ready for Able Team. The idea was that Lyons and crew would arrive in Miami, find the van and be ready for business.

"Did he ever say what the business was?" interrupted Lyons.

"I'll get to that. In a word, yes."

The business, as described by Brognola, was the termination—with extreme prejudice—of Danny Forbes's killers.

Due to the time pressure, Kurtzman hadn't been able to use sources he would normally employ to assemble the equipment. So he and Brognola had arranged through the DEA and a contact of Hal's to put things together for them.

Normally they wouldn't use that approach. Never trust anybody, was Brognola's unwritten rule. But this time they had broken that rule. It should have been safe enough, and nine times out of ten it would have been. In this case, however, fate had intervened.

Quite by accident, Hal's friend had delegated the task to the agent under suspicion.

It had been a classic case of security causing miscommunication. Brognola knew of the investigation and who the agent under suspicion was. But Hal's friend, the agent's immediate supervisor in fact, did not. So he had delegated the task to precisely that person.

This particular agent—supposedly completely trustworthy—had asked a few questions, then arranged for the van.

Gadgets shook his head as he told the story. "I wonder why it's always the 'completely trustworthy' ones?" he muttered to nobody in particular.

Lyons shrugged. "Good cover," he said simply. "That's what being a good spy or double agent is all about."

When the van blew, Lucero's insider was nailed. Immediate steps were taken to plug the leak.

"You should have heard the chief," said Gadgets, laughing. "He said, in that booming way he has, 'Great job, Schwarz. Hell, that guy wasn't even your target. We'll have to do this more often, set you up as bait and see who bites!' "

"What'd you say?" asked Blancanales.

"I told him we should get a bonus for plugging the leak. He didn't seem too anxious to do that, so I decided to check into the best hotel I could find. Sort of as compensation, you might say."

"I like your style, Homes."

Gadgets became serious. "Actually, this one just seemed like a good, safe place to hole up."

Lyons nodded and poured some more Scotch. "So, what else did he say?"

Gadgets thought back on it.

A new van and equipment would be forthcoming. Hopefully, it would be put together by more reliable folk. No surprises this time. Able Team was to catch some sleep and be ready for action the next morning.

"Or today, actually," Gadgets added, checking his watch.

"And in the meantime?" asked Lyons.

"In the meantime, they'll try to locate the target for us."

"And then?"

Gadgets's face split into a wide grin. "You should have heard him, Homes. It was great."

"How so, amigo?" inquired Blancanales.

"Well, you know how he will sometimes talk in bureaucratese, talking like he's being really formal, only phony formal? Real serious, like it was in some memo?"

The other two men nodded.

"Well, he was at his best here. He said..." Gadgets closed his eyes and thought. "He said something pretty close to this.

"'Gadgets, me lad,'" he said. "'Gadgets, our legal system, for all its faults, is the best in the world. That is appropriate, because this country is the best in the world. But, in order to work, it makes one very important assumption. Do you know what that is, Gadgets?'

"I said I didn't. So he told me.

"'Why, it assumes that people won't kill off the witnesses. Hell, go to trial if you're a crook—that's well and good. If some idiot jury wants to let them off, so be it. But for Pete's sake, don't kill off the witnesses.

"'When you kill the witnesses, you undermine the entire legal system. Why? Because it works. Killing the witnesses just plain works. Can't prosecute a case without witnesses. And when one guy does it, others will see that it works. The word gets out. And pretty soon they'll all do it.'"

Gadgets looked at them and grinned.

"And then do you know what he said?"

Without waiting for a reply Schwarz took a deep breath and continued.

"He said, 'And that would mean the end of America as we know it. The end of a way of life. Do you want that, Gadgets? Do you think I want that?'

"So what do we do, Chief, I asked," Gadgets continued. "And he says, 'Why, kill him, of course.' And he hung up."

Lyons, too, was smiling by this time.

"Sounds like the chief was unusually direct and to the point," he observed. "There must be other cases where they're afraid this will happen, unless we send a message."

Gadgets nodded. "I think that's it exactly," he agreed. "Send a message."

Lyons looked at the time. It was after two in the morning, 02:10 to be exact.

"Well," he said. "Orders is orders. I think I'll try to grab some sleep. And then tomorrow—" he hesitated, then grinned again "—why, tomorrow we'll go out and defend the American way of life."

17

Brognola had been as good as his word.

The three men slept only a few hours. At six-thirty they arose and got ready. At 07:10 the telephone rang, and it was Brognola.

"West lot. Right now. Man with a tan Dodge van." He read off the license plate. "He'll be waiting there for you, and no, there won't be any surprises this time."

"How will we know him?"

"You won't. He's an irregular."

Lyons realized that even if the man had assembled the van and gear, the enemy could have taken the guy out and substituted their own. Along with another "surprise," of course.

"So how do we establish him as the genuine article, if you'll pardon the paranoia, Hal?"

"Standard recognition code is authorized and expected. If he knows the code, you're ten-four."

"And if he doesn't?"

"If he doesn't, you're authorized to shoot him if you'd like. How's that?"

Gadgets, who could hear the conversation due to Brognola's booming voice, whispered to Lyons. "How about if we just make him open it up?"

"Who?"

"The irregular."

Lyons relayed the suggestion to Brognola. The big Fed's reply was short and to the point. "If you like."

Can't do much better than that, thought Lyons. Aloud he said, "You locate our target?"

"Negative. But we're working on it. First things first. Go check out the van, make sure the equipment is adequate. Then get something to eat and stand by."

"Roger."

They found the man, and they found the van. The identification code was made and confirmed, and the man did in fact open the van for them.

There were no surprises.

He was one of the cadre of "trusted irregulars," located all over the world. The term had originally been supplied by Gadgets. It was borrowed from history books and meant citizen volunteers who were willing to assist on the battle lines.

Like their Revolutionary War forefathers, the "irregulars" were not full-time soldiers or full-time operatives for Stony Man Farm. Instead, most were men and women with regular jobs, who could be called upon for special, short-term assistance should the need arise.

One didn't apply to become an "irregular."

The selection was made informally on a case to case basis. It generally came about when a potential candidate came to the attention of somebody who was in a position to drop a name to Brognola. Time permitting, Hal would have the person checked out and cautious inquiries would be made.

They came from all walks of life.

Sales personnel, telephone company employees, gym operators, weapons enthusiasts, students, construction workers, warehouse employees, grocery store clerks. Many of them—though qualified and approved—would never be called upon. And if they did happen to draw an assignment, the one single overriding consideration was their ability to keep their mouths shut about it.

Security. Always security.

The man touched his baseball cap. "Have fun," he said simply.

Then he was gone, trudging across the parking lot to the hotel. He would catch a cab and go back to his job. There was a good chance he would never know exactly what the mission involved. Of course, if he was sharp and read the papers he might be able to guess, especially if things got real exciting.

Lyons also knew that Brognola made a practice of sending somebody around to talk to the irregular after the mission was over.

He did this for a variety of reasons. It gave the guy a general idea about what the task had been about, why it was important. They also did it to reiterate the need for security and to pay a fee for their assistance.

A surprising number of them declined to accept it.

The three men surveyed the contents of the van. At first glance it looked as if a bunch of salesmen or businessmen had tossed their briefcases inside.

A standard Samsonite attaché case, molded gray plastic with a crinkle-textured finish, housed an Uzi machine pistol.

Sort of, anyway.

It resembled the standard Uzi pistol sold to the U.S. There were two important differences, however. First, it was chambered for .45 ACP, rather than the standard 9 mm. Second, it had a selector switch for fully automatic as well as the standard semiauto fire.

A descendant of the original Uzi machine gun developed by the Israelis in the 1950s, the pistol had many of the same features. The number-one consideration was that it work—work well, work reliably, work every time. Sand and salt and being dropped mustn't affect it.

Looks came secondary.

The result had been a squatty, functional weapon. An uninitiated observer who viewed it from the side would think it resembled a fat T.

The receiver and barrel—the horizontal bar of the T—were housed in businesslike stamped metal. The bulky pistol grip jutted straight downward from just off the center of the wide part of the receiver, forming the vertical part of the T.

In short, it was all business.

The Uzi pistol wasn't available commercially in .45, although there was every indication that it would soon be. And it certainly wasn't available in an ''autoburn'' model. Where Brognola, or John ''Cowboy'' Kissinger, had managed to procure this one was a mystery.

Lyons had fired one on several occasions, back at the farm. Kissinger had obtained it to see what the others thought of it.

It took some skill to fire on full-automatic. It also took a sturdy grip and forearm to hold it. And even with that, short bursts, two to four rounds, were the order of the day.

There were two of them, one for Lyons and one for Blancanales.

A similar attaché case held a MAC-10. Gadgets was partial to the MAC-10, and Lyons noted that its briefcase even had the initials "HS" on it. A nice touch, he thought, either by the irregular or by Brognola.

"Here you are, Hermann," he said, passing it over, winking as he used Gadgets's given name.

"Thanks, Homes," Gadgets responded dryly.

They scanned the rest of the gear.

In addition to the handguns—though both the Uzi and the MAC-10 weren't really pistols but were actually ultrashort assault weapons, to Lyons's way of thinking—Brognola had included three more .45 Government Model pistols, three M-16's with full-auto capability and three sawed-off shotguns.

The latter was intriguing. They looked like regular pump shotguns, except that the stock ended just behind the pistol grip. Loaded with double 0 buck, they made a relatively concealable and highly maneuverable "kick ass and take no prisoners" weapon.

It would be fitting, somehow, if he could nail Lalo with double 0, Lyons thought. After all, that was what the Cuban had narrowly escaped back in the National City warehouse at the hands of McMurray.

A blanket covered something else in the van. Lyons moved it aside.

Underneath lay a long, rectangular black suitcase. It had a corrugated leatherlike finish and metal protectors on all corners.

A gold metal tag approximately two by three inches was attached near the plastic carrying handle. Engraved on the tag were the words "Optical equipment—telescope, property Harold Laboratories." A similar message appeared on a larger sticker pasted to each side of the case.

Harold Laboratories, thought Lyons. Cute. "Hal" was the short version of "Harold."

They opened it up.

Inside, carefully encased in foam, were the pieces to a weapon that Blancanales recognized instantly. He let out a low whistle of appreciation.

"All ri-i-ight," he said softly.

The weapon was a Barrett M-82, a .50-caliber semiautomatic rifle designed to fire the .50 Browning machine-gun round.

Though not a machine gun—it was semiauto only—the M-82 provided awesome firepower.

The .50-caliber round would take out a car or chop through cement walls in seconds. The projectile weighed in at 750 grains or somewhere around one and three-quarter ounces. That made it some five to seven times as heavy as a standard .38 special slug. With a muzzle velocity of over twenty-eight hundred feet per second, the muzzle energy was in the vicinity of twelve thousand foot/pounds.

Not twelve hundred. Twelve thousand.

Like twenty or twenty-five times as much as even a fairly hot pistol load. The weapon came with a bipod for stability, an eleven-round magazine and a ten-power scope.

"Think this'll stop a Ferrari?" Gadgets inquired facetiously, his voice soft.

Blancanales winked. "It just might, Homes. It just might." He paused, then added, "With any luck, we just might get a chance to find out."

18

Sometimes, reflected Lyons, they just give it to you. Almost on a silver platter.

Of course, this wasn't quite like that.

All that had been given to them was the place and time. It was still up to them to make the kill, without getting themselves shot to shit. That might not be so hard in other circumstances. But in the middle of a city, where stray civilians could easily walk into the fire zone, it presented some problems.

Like you couldn't just call in an air strike, then move up and shoot anything that was still kicking.

Too bad. That would be one neat way to do it.

Brognola's call had come within minutes of their return to the room. Through his ties in the Justice Department, and because their mission had evidently been sanctioned at the highest levels, he was able to give them the where, when and what. And, hopefully, who.

It would be up to Able Team to supply the how.

The "where" was opposite a strip of beach south of downtown Miami. The "when" was that evening, sometime after eight, according to the informant. The "what" was a midsize drug deal. Lalo would be riding shotgun, making sure nobody got cute.

''Midsize'' was a relative term.

The deal was for three kilos or a little over nine and a half pounds. The product, Peruvian flake, was still one of the finest cocaines money could buy. Pure, or nearly so.

In a normal sense, it was a major deal. Huge, in fact. This quantity signified that a major wholesaler had stocked up, to supply his own lower-level distributors. It was midsize only in the sense that it was only a fraction of what the importer—none other than Roman Lucero, himself—would bring in in a single shipment.

It was still enough to kill and be killed over.

This was so from the perspective of both the buyer and the seller. Each side would have armed guards, ''gunsels,'' at the transaction. Each side would be edgy and nervous. Lyons had been there—he'd made undercover buys as a narcotics officer, and he knew the feeling.

It wasn't just the feeling of getting caught.

Sure, no dealer wanted to be arrested. But far more than that was the concern about the other party.

The constant fear to those involved in the deal was that it was a setup, that one side or the other would try for a ''rip'' or a ''burn.'' That meant killing the other side and making off with both the money and the dope.

It had happened more than once.

For that reason a lot of deals were arranged to take place—were ''set up to go down,'' so to speak—in public places. The presence of civilians helped deter the burn.

It also ruled out a lot of very efficient, and spectacular, ways of terminating Lalo. With extreme prejudice, of course.

After Brognola ran down the where, when and what, Lyons gave it some thought. The "how" was what concerned him. How can we take these guys out with minimum risk to Mom and Pop and the kids at the beach?

"I'll need a Ferrari, Chief," he said abruptly into the phone.

He might as well have said he wanted Air Force One or the Challenger or a third arm. A long silence was his only reply.

"Or a Lamborghini or something equivalent," the Ironman persisted.

"Why?" Brognola's voice was icy.

"Backup. That's all. If something goes to shit, we'll need something as fast as what he's got. Unless you want us to just stand back and nuke the whole place, of course. Drop the big one and sort the bodies out later."

"Can you drive one of those things? You don't just get behind the wheel and put it in 'drive,' you know."

"Is a frog's ass watertight?" Lyons retorted.

The upshot of it was that by six, Gadgets and Blancanales were in the van. A few spaces away, Lyons waited in the Lamborghini, a sleek, silver-gray missile with an instrument panel like an aircraft.

I wonder if Julie would like to ride in this, he thought, then pushed the image abruptly from his mind.

Forget Julie, he commanded himself.

The area consisted of a strip of beach some thirty feet wide. A wide sidewalk bordered the beach. Inland from the sidewalk was a strip of grass that varied between fifteen and thirty feet wide.

Palm trees grew along the grassy strip, slender spears that jutted upward and fanned out at the top.

Beyond the grass was a parking lot, a vast expanse of pavement that led to Bayshore Drive.

A smattering of cars dotted the parking lot. Parked in the midst of them was the Dodge van. Lyons and the Lamborghini were only a few spaces away.

The van had a special periscope mounted into the ventilation hatch on its roof. Gadgets and Blancanales took turns on watch. They communicated with Lyons via a set of hand-held radios, each tuned to a special tactical frequency.

They waited.

Inside the van, sweat beaded on their skin. The beads reached critical size and ran downward. Even their loose-fitting casual shirts grew wet. Droplets stained the waistbands of their trousers. Others fell to the carpet.

Lyons, wearing casual, stylish clothes and Wayfarer-style sunglasses, leaned back in the seat of the Lamb. Beside him, under a beach towel, was the Uzi pistol and three spare clips. In the passenger foot-well was another Uzi, this one the long model or regular machine gun.

A sudden comparison amused him. The Lamborghini. Lamb, for short. Lamb, as in sheep. And, inside it, Lyons, the killer, armed to the teeth. Lyons, the lone wolf.

Lyons in the Lamb. A wolf in the Lamb. A wolf in sheep's clothing.

Poetic bastard, he thought.

Seconds ticked into minutes. Minutes dragged into quarter hours.

Shortly after eight a red Porsche pulled into the lot. It made a full circle sweep of the vast surface, then pulled to a stop some fifty or sixty yards away, as far from any other vehicles as possible.

Two men got out. They, too, wore casual clothes and sunglasses. Each carried a canvas bag, which they dropped to the ground as they lounged against the car and scanned the lot.

Ten minutes later a finely tuned growl pushed through the evening air. Without having to look Lyons knew it would be the Ferrari.

The sleek black car made its own circuit of the lot. Finally it slid to a stop next to the Porsche.

Inside the Ferrari was a dark-complected man and a blond woman in a low cut dress. Even at that distance Lyons could see she had been made for low cut.

A brief exchange occurred between the men by the Porsche and the man in the Ferrari. Then, abruptly, the Ferrari backed away. It made a small semicircle and came to a stop, parallel to the Porsche but fifty feet away.

Side by side but fifty feet between them.

A long, dark blue Continental slid noiselessly into the lot. It drove to a spot almost midway between the Porsche and the Ferrari and stopped.

Moments later a black Cadillac pulled in next to the Continental. The Caddie faced the opposite direction, so that its passenger side was next to the passenger side of the Continental.

The driver's side of the Continental was thus some fifteen or twenty feet from the Porsche. The driver's side of the Caddie was an equal distance from the Ferrari.

Lyons looked at the four vehicles across the lot. Porsche, Continental, Caddie, Ferrari. Very slick, he thought appreciatively. Very slick, indeed.

The deal would go down between the people in the two big cars. It would take place in the area between those two vehicles. And, for security, each side had its "gunsels" in a fast car nearby.

A major narcotics transaction, white death being dealt under the palms, against the pink-and-blue skies of sunset.

A beautiful place to be, and to live. And maybe to die.

He would be willing to bet that the gunmen in the Porsche did not belong to the men in Continental, which was closest to the Porsche. Likewise, Lalo, or whoever it was in the Ferrari, did not work for the men in the Caddie.

These guys took no chances.

The arrangement meant that each side had to expose its driver to possible gunfire from the other side's henchmen. It made for a hell of an incentive not to try to do a "burn" or a "let's see if we can get *both* the money *and* the coke" kind of caper.

Sort of the dope dealer's functional equivalent of an escrow, the Ironman thought.

He watched and waited.

Nothing happened.

For some reason it didn't look like the deal was going down. Suddenly, without warning, the sharp staccato sound of gunfire shattered the evening stillness. Orange flashes danced from the men by the four cars.

Lyons could see the flames. Straight on.

An instant later, just as he was starting to react, another sound reached his ears. It was the rapid clanking of slugs striking metal.

The metal was their van.

19

Lyons wrenched the door handle on the Lamborghini, then kicked the door open. As he did so, he reached for the Uzi carbine, then dived onto the pavement.

A metallic clanging reached his ears as bullets struck the van, several spaces to his right.

No time to think what had gone wrong.

He rolled to one side, behind an old Plymouth in the next space. The survival techniques were automatic, because he had practiced them for untold hours.

Cover and concealment.

Two similar concepts to the commando. But "similar" did not mean they were the same thing. In fact, a vast difference existed between the two. Concealment hid, cover protected. A bush could be used for concealment. A boulder was cover. If a bullet can go through it, it ain't cover.

If the warrior was lucky, he got cover. Sometimes, though, concealment was the best he could hope for.

A car could be cover, Lyons knew, except for getting his feet shot off beneath it. But there was an answer to that, too, at least a partial one. He knew from his cop days that a tire would stop or deflect a lot of slugs, all except the real high-speed stuff. Accordingly with a skill borne of hours of training, he moved forward to a position right behind the front wheel.

Drawing a deep breath as he crouched, he tried to get a feel for the fire.

No slugs hit the Plymouth, yet the clanging of projectiles against steel continued. They still haven't made me, he thought. They must be concentrating on the van.

No time like the present, as his high school football coach used to say.

The folding stock on the carbine locked into place with two clicks, and he was ready.

Turn off the TV set. And now, up and over, Ironman.

Just nut up and do it.

He rose to a crouch and brought the carbine over the flat metal surface of the hood of the Plymouth. As long as you've got the vehicle for cover, no hip-shooting—keep your body low over the car's body and sight down the barrels he schooled himself. Sight as best you can, that is, given the iron "battle sights" of the carbine, the fact that it wasn't a sharp-shooting weapon and the fact that no matter how many times you've done it before, your guts are turning flip-flops on you.

Across the lot, the orange flashes from the men by the four cars made nice aiming points. Christ, there had to be at least six or seven men with guns—where had they all come from?

Teeth clenched, Lyons clamped down on the trigger and held it there. After all, he thought, that's what a trigger is for, isn't it?

Until the damn thing's empty or jams or the barrel gets too hot, that is.

The carbine bucked in his grip.

Explosions from gunfire mingled with the flat metallic clacking of the Uzi's bolt, blowing open and slamming shut on a new round. Strangely, Lyons could even detect a much more delicate sound despite the racket—the clinking of cartridge cases against the car next to him and the tinkle as they dropped to the pavement.

The jerking of the weapon meant he had to concentrate on the silhouettes of the men behind the winks of orange of their weapons. Otherwise he would lose them, either in his own muzzle-flash or behind the bucking barrel or frame of the Uzi.

He pulled the metal stock in tight against his shoulder. The Uzi's recoil was negligible, compared to many weapons. It was more of a persistent heavy vibration—a sort of shaking, actually—than a real recoil.

Dose, he thought suddenly.

"Dose" was a good word for it. Especially since these men were drug dealers. A dose, or in pharmaceutical terms, "dosage unit," was a quantitative term—how much to take or how much to give, depending on which end you were.

Have a dose of Uzi, assholes.

Take as prescribed by your doctor. Dr. Lyons, that is. Have some .45-caliber dosage units.

Dr. Carl's miracle cure for the drug problem. One treatment prevented recurrence.

He held it on the targets on the right, the Porsche, for a good, long dose. Then he shifted to the left, to give them a dose, too.

Even as he concentrated on his new targets, Lyons was aware that some of his shots had struck home. One of the men spun around and dropped to the pavement. Another staggered. Good shooting, Iron-man, he thought. He had "felt" that those rounds were right on target—sometimes that happened, times when he knew even as bullet left muzzle that it had hit, or missed. All marksmen had experienced the feeling, Lyons knew, a peculiar unity of man and weapon.

In his peripheral vision he saw one of the men he had hit suddenly leap onto the hood of the Caddie. Before his brain had a chance to analyze it, though, something made a flat, smacking sound nearby.

Very nearby, indeed.

The Plymouth's windshield turned into a mass of irregular lines as cracks radiated out from where two slugs impacted. Small bits of glass stung his face.

Suddenly the clanging was much more immediate.

"Shit!"

The oath tore from his throat in a gutteral snarl as he clenched his teeth and held on to the bucking ma-chine gun. He knew gritting the teeth and snarling wouldn't stop the onrushing slugs. Still, it was an automatic response.

Snarl at the attackers. Growl as you charge.

Lyons did it without thinking, part of some primi-tive, fight-mode response built into man centuries ago.

He heard himself doing it.

The thought flashes through his mind—must remember to ask Gadgets about that sometime, but shit why am I thinking about this crap in the middle of a firefight?

Something hit the tire he was crouched behind. He felt, or heard the impact, a heavy bump, as though someone had pounded the tire with a hammer. Then more hammering, close and loud, and he knew they had his location for sure. Hell, if he could aim at their muzzle-flashes they could aim at his, hey, no fair, you assholes. . . .

Something smacked his shoulder, hot and hard.

At the same moment the Uzi clacked empty, the last round gone, the barrel too hot to touch. Lyons recoiled and ducked behind the car. He turned his back to the fender and wheel and slid into a sitting position, feeling the hot blood flow down his arm and down his side.

An instant later the growl of the Ferrari's engine reached his ears.

INSIDE THE VAN, Blancanales had sensed it coming.

"Look out!" he warned Gadgets.

"What is it?"

"We've been burned!"

Even as he was speaking, the figures by the four cars were moving into action. And it was an action that unified them. For the moment they had forgotten their mutual distrust of one another—here was a common enemy. Whoever had caused the enemy to be there could be dealt with later.

The back doors of both the Caddie and the Continental swung open. Two men clambered out of each car and scurried to cover behind the cars.

Each man held something dark and businesslike in his hands. Somehow, the Politician didn't think the objects were umbrellas or electric drills.

Orange flashes suddenly winked from the area of the four cars. An instant later the sharp sound of automatic gunfire reached the Able Team warriors.

An instant after that the slugs found their target.

The clanging of bullets against the van's steel body was deafening. A jackhammer held against the frame would have produced the same effect. Inside the van, the effect felt like being inside a drum when a drumroll was called for.

"Shit!" Gadgets shouted.

"Dios!" breathed Blancanales fervently.

The van was parked at an angle to the drug dealers. The front corner of the driver's side pointed toward the four cars. A sliding door opened on the right side of the Dodge. Lyons and the Lamborghini were several spaces to the left.

Glass showered them as the windshield shattered in a hail of lead.

By flattening himself against the left wall of the van, Blancanales could get a straight shot at their attackers. It meant shooting through the cracked windshield, around the upright back of the driver's seat.

He started to grab one of the Uzis, then said to hell with it and grabbed an M-16 instead.

"Cover your ears!" he shouted unnecessarily, flashing a quick grin.

The commotion became thunderous. Hot brass bounced off the confined interior of the van as the Politician fired controlled bursts of autoburn.

By the four cars, the flickering of muzzle-flashes became more ragged. One of the gunsels spun around and doubled up, as if folding his body around the shock of the impacts. A second one ducked behind his car, apparently deciding discretion was indeed the better part of valor.

Blancanales started to shift his aim to one of the other men. Before he settled on target, though, the man staggered awkwardly. Clearly he had just taken multiple hits.

Lyons! thought the Politician excitedly.

The Ironman must be out of the Lamborghini, laying down some fire of his own.

Still, it was too late for the Politician's brain to cancel the order. Even as Blancanales was realizing that his partner had already punched the gunsel's ticket, the M-16 was steadying on the staggering man and the trigger finger was contracting.

Two to the head; the rest of the burst missed.

The man's body was flung across the hood of the Caddie, hurled there by the impact of the bullets. Blood and brains spattered on the windshield. Bright crimson rivulets streamed downward.

The sound of metal sliding on metal reached the Politician, despite the thunderous din inside the van. Even without looking he knew that Gadgets had slid the side door to the van open.

A quick glance confirmed it. His Able Team partner scurried out. He dropped down outside the van, with something long—real long—in his hands. He half dashed, half dived off to the right, behind the car two spaces away.

Blancanales realized that Gadgets had the Barrett M-82, the .50-caliber rifle, in his hands.

Over five feet and thirty-five pounds of firepower.

At that moment a motor roared to life across the lot, and the Continental started to move.

20

Tires screeched on the pavement as the Continental roared forward. Blue smoke rose from behind the wheels.

From his position on the ground Gadgets saw the massive sedan accelerate. Time to try out the new toy, he thought.

Actually he wouldn't have even considered going into a firefight with a weapon he didn't know how to operate, and operate well. In this instance he and Blancanales had both fired the M-82 before.

Besides, apart from its size, it was basically like any other semiauto rifle in terms of operation.

He had assembled it in the van, while they had been waiting for the narcotics dealers to arrive.

The damn thing was nearly five and a half feet long.

It resembled an oversize M-16 in appearance. It was what would result, say, if an M-16 got an overdose of radiation and mutated. Make the combat rifle some fifty percent again as long, much of the extra length from the receiver forward. Add a bipod midway down the steel stock.

In order to accommodate the massive .50-caliber machine gun bullets, the clip had to undergo a major expansion. Instead of the forward-curving device on the M-16, this had a slanting, boxlike clip that jutted down just in front of the pistol grip and trigger guard.

Using the fire from Blancanales and Lyons as cover, Schwarz ducked behind a nearby station wagon, lugging the massive cannon with him.

Prone, he inched forward.

The front wheel of the station wagon provided some cover. Gadgets eased the rifle around until the barrel pointed at the four cars. Low to the ground as he was, they made rectangular shapes against the pink sky.

The Continental continued its sharp acceleration forward.

Gadgets dumped the three clips on the pavement next to him. Each held eleven rounds. Eleven at 750 grains per, meant that a pound or so of bullets would have been launched with every full clip he went through.

In one of the clips, the rounds had red tips. In one, the rounds were black-tipped, except that the first, fourth and eighth had red tips. In the third, all the tips were the basic jacketed color.

The basic rounds were just that. No frills, nothing extra, just a hell of a potent, ass-hauling bullet.

The red-tipped ones were tracers. The black tips were armor piercing.

Gadgets picked up the black-and-red combo and slid the clip into place. He wiggled it, then felt it "clack" into the proper position. Then he closed the bolt.

The Continental picked up speed.

It came at an angle, heading generally toward him but also going from left to right across his field of fire.

He could see the driver inside, bending over, keeping low.

Gadgets shifted his position to the left, rotating the muzzle on the bipod. He didn't even try to use the scope at this range but, instead, sighted along the barrel.

Boom!

The straight stock slammed back against his shoulder. Strangely, the kick, though substantial, was not as much as he had expected the first time he fired it. Some of the big-bore elephant guns, for instance, kicked worse.

He felt the rifle rotate along its length in his hands. It was almost as if the weapon were alive and shifting its weight to one leg of the bipod.

Bullet torque, he had heard the experts call it.

The barrel had rifling, the grooves cut along the inside in a spiral. The rifling made the bullet twist, turning along an axis that ran from tip to base of the projectile. The result was added stability in flight.

Of course, the laws of physics work even in this context.

There is nothing that automatically says the bullet must do the twisting. It is only the fact that the slug has so little mass compared with the barrel that causes it rather than the weapon to do the turning. But the forces are still there.

With a bullet as damn big as a .50 caliber going down a rifle barrel, the forces trying to twist the barrel—at the same time the barrel is trying to twist the bullet—are noticeable.

Bullet torque.

Even as the report from the shot was dying out, he heard the solid clank of the projectile striking home. Instantly the car swerved sharply.

Straight toward him.

He had expected it to swerve away from him, assuming it changed course at all. It didn't make sense to turn toward the gunfire, although it was an old Navy trick to chase the splashes of shells that missed your ship, on the theory that any correction would thereby be an *over*correction.

But, though Gadgets was familiar with the "chase your splashes" routine, he didn't think of it. All the Stony Man warrior could think of was that the Continental must be trying to run him over.

Tortured rubber clawed at the pavement, accompanied by a sharp screech. The car swayed on its soft suspension from the change in direction.

It looked as if it were going to come around, and make a sharp arc, so it could head right at him.

Gadgets had aimed at the front of the passenger's door. He figured that would be enough leading for where he wanted the bullet to strike. It was a guesstimate only, based on experience and feel.

Marksmen called it "Kentucky windage." Gadgets, with his scientific approach to everything, knew the concept well.

Technically, the term meant a rough estimate of the amount a shooter had to shoot to one side of the target to compensate for a crosswind. The wind would blow a bullet sideways in a "drift." Kentucky windage was the amount a shooter had to aim to the upwind side of the target to compensate for that drift.

However, over time the phrase grew to be used in a more general sense.

In that manner, it also applied to adjustments for moving targets, where the target was traveling from one side to the other across the field of fire. So used, Kentucky windage meant the amount the shooter had to aim ahead so that the target would "run into" the bullet.

Gadgets estimated that if he shot for the front edge of the front car door—the crack that separated the door from the fender—the slug would strike the door midway.

Just even with where the driver would be.

As it turned out, he couldn't have estimated it better. He was right on target.

Dead on, in fact.

The heavy bullet went through the steel door like it was cardboard. It hit the driver in the right side. The entry wound was just under the armpit. The bullet shattered all but three of his ribs and blew his spine out the left side of his body. Then it continued through the driver's door and probably fell way the hell out in the ocean somewhere.

When the bullet struck the driver lurched to his right, bending around the force of the impact. That jerked the wheel—and thus the car itself—to his right, as well.

Toward Gadgets, in other words.

The Able Team commando remembered only too well what it felt like to play matador to a charging Ferrari. He'd be goddamned if he was going to let it happen again.

"Fuck you-u-u!" he screamed as the car bore down on him.

He fired four more rounds at the onrushing car, just as fast as he could work the bolt.

As the second or third one hit—he couldn't say for sure which—the car suddenly locked its wheels and went into a skid. The tires screeched on the pavement and slid toward him.

Gadgets started to roll to one side. Then his computerlike brain said he didn't have to.

He bet his life on it.

And won. The massive vehicle screeched to a halt ten feet in front of him.

Much later the experts would learn what happened. They would find out that one of the armor-piercing rounds had entered the drive train on the onrushing car. It had traveled the length of the drive shaft, bouncing around here and there, of course. It tore the shit out of two or three critical gears and generally jammed the thing to a total freeze that resulted in the final skid.

The Able Team commando was not too proud to let out a sigh of relief. He gave the massive rifle an affectionate pat in the breach area, by the bolt.

"Nice shooting, Old Betsy."

LYONS GRITTED HIS TEETH as he shoved a fresh clip into the Uzi. Then he inched forward and peered around the front of the Plymouth.

Nothing moved around the three cars where the dope deal had so abruptly aborted.

The gunfire from the van stopped.

Lyons peered ahead, squinting in the blinding light caused by the setting sun.

Still no movement.

"Pol!" He rasped the name.

"*Sí*, amigo?"

"You okay?"

"*Sí*, amigo."

"Where's Gadgets?"

The third Able Team member answered for himself. "Over here!"

"You code four?"

"Yep. No sweat."

Lyons let out a sigh of relief. His partners were all alive and well. Or alive anyway; "well" would have to wait for further data.

The firefight had been brief and terrifying.

It was always like that in real life, Lyons knew. Adrenaline charged your body with inhuman strength, but it didn't make you bulletproof. The sight of orange flashes from gun muzzles pointed at you was unforgettable. No matter how well you "turned off the television set," your body was always braced for it—the smack of a slug striking home against your own flesh.

A minute went by, then another. The faint wall of the first sirens, still very far away, reached their ears.

"Let's move in! Cover me!" Lyons hissed.

He got to his feet and circled forward, Uzi clamped against his side. The wound hurt but wasn't incapacitating. If anything, it made him feel more alive.

You can't feel pain if you're dead, he thought. Pain means you're alive. Besides, it was a long way from his heart.

Behind him, Gadgets and Blancanales grouped to cover him. Blancanales had abandoned the M-16 in favor of one of the shotguns; Gadgets now had his MAC-10.

Suddenly something moved between the cars.

Lalo—it had to be him—flashed from the Caddie toward the Ferrari. He had a gun in his hand, a Walther, Lyons guessed. He had come out of nowhere and moved like a cat.

Lyons was just as quick. It was time to effect the termination.

"Die, fucker!" Lyons roared the battle cry as he swung the Uzi at Lalo.

An instant later he swung it away again.

The Cuban had grabbed a woman by the arm and was hauling her out of the car. The briefcase she gripped struck the body of the Ferrari and came open.

Bags of white powder fell to the pavement.

It was impossible to fire at Lalo without hitting the woman.

Using the woman as a shield, the Cuban had somehow gotten inside the Ferrari. The movement was so quick the eye couldn't follow it. "Bad magic," Danny Forbes had called it in his letter. The car roared into life, Lalo behind the wheel, his left arm out of the window around the neck of the blond woman.

A high, maniacal laugh came from the Ferrari. The race car leaped forward. The blond woman was jerked from her feet by the viselike forearm that held her. She was dragged along for some forty yards until Lalo let her go.

Without waiting for the others Lyons sprinted for the Lamborghini.

Then something caught his eye, and he altered his course a couple of degrees to grab it.

It was the M-82, Gadgets's "Old Betsy," leaning against the van, on the side closest to the Lamborghini. Gadgets must have left it there when he took the MAC-10 for the approach.

Lyons grabbed the monstrous weapon. He hurled it through the open passenger window of the Lamborghini, then vaulted over the hood of the car and climbed in the driver's side.

The Ferrari was already leaving the lot and turning onto Bayshore Drive. With a squeal of rubber the Lamborghini raced after it, pulling out onto the road as the Ferrari's black shape dwindled ahead of them.

Within the first mile Lyons realized there was something wrong with the car.

"Oh, no," he groaned. A slug from the firefight must have hit it and done some crippling though not immediately incapacitating damage, he thought.

He put his foot to the floor as he ran the car up through the gears.

Injured though it was, the Lamb was something to behold, he thought. The speedometer needle reached one-seventy as they shot along the arrow-straight road that was strangely empty of traffic.

The Ferrari was now only a hundred yards ahead. Suddenly its brake lights came on.

At the same moment the Lamborghini gave a terminal shudder and died. Lyons stood on the brakes, and the sleek silver arrow slid on a screeching, smoking trail of burning rubber. He fought to control it and won, thanks to the superb engineering of the car. For a couple of bad moments he wondered if he was going to rear-end the Ferrari.

Then, abruptly, the black car leaped ahead, passing an impromptu caravan of three motor homes that had caused Lalo to brake in the first place.

Lyons knew that his quarry would be history, unless . . .

The Ironman yanked the steering wheel of his skidding vehicle hard left, taking his foot off the brake as he did so. The car shot across the oncoming lane, onto the far shoulder.

From this angle he could see the Ferrari as it roared into the distance.

Lyons bailed out of the Lamborghini, dragging the M-82 out with him. From a position behind the race car, he manhandled the massive gun onto the roof. Despite the circumstances he couldn't help feeling a pang of regret as the steel legs of the bipod gouged the silver-gray finish.

He estimated the range at four hundred yards. No, make that five, going on six. A quarter of a mile, closing on a half.

The scope settled on the Ferrari. He found the image. The picture was there. No "Kentucky windage" or "leading" was necessary, since the Ferrari was going virtually straight away from him.

Steady. No movement of the sight picture. Pressure on the trigger.

The massive rifle fired, driving a railroad spike of pain into his wounded shoulder.

Nearly a half mile ahead, the Ferrari flipped abruptly off the road. It rolled over and over along the shoulder, showers of sparks flying at irregular intervals along its path as steel struck pavement.

Lyons traced its progress in the scope. Finally it came to a stop, ironically, on all four wheels.

Adrenaline coursing through him, the Ironman half expected it to drive off again.

It didn't.

Then something moved in the edge of the narrow field of the scope's view. It was way back from the car, and Lyons almost didn't see it.

A dark shape. A human shape, pushing itself to its feet in the ditch, a hundred feet back from where the car now rested.

Lyons shifted the scope back. The figure turned toward him.

Lalo!

He let the cross hairs settle on the staggering target. Make this a good one, Ironman, he thought.

For a massive vise that could squeeze a man's brains out.

For Danny Forbes, the sucker who had never really gotten an even break. For all the other men and women you have tortured and killed. For all the human breakage—the lives and loves ruined by the white powder whose commerce you have helped.

For Julie.

For me.

The massive rifle slammed into his shoulder a second time.

Better than an ounce and a half of bullet. Twenty-eight hundred fps. Twelve thousand foot-pounds of energy at the muzzle—so it's down to "only" ten thousand at that range.

Termination accomplished.

With extreme prejudice.

As the rifle finished its unique twisting recoil, Lyons found the spot where Lalo had been standing. He wasn't standing there any longer. The human shape on the ground lay at not-quite-human angles, as though every bone in its body had been shattered.

Grimly the Ironman lowered the rifle and spoke out loud, although there was nobody around to hear him.

"Bad magic, my ass."

EPILOGUE

The wound to his shoulder proved to be of the "treated and released" variety.

That is to say, the doctors insisted he stay overnight in the hospital. "For observation." When Lyons pointed out they didn't have enough manpower to accomplish that, the doctors changed it to "treated and released."

Blancanales wasn't with him at the hospital.

The Politician had stayed behind to make the report to Stony Man Farm. Gadgets had driven Lyons to the hospital, then had telephoned Blancanales while the doctors did their job. It was just after midnight when they managed to get away.

Back at the Marriott, Gadgets had broken away from his partner as they crossed the lobby. Lyons waited as he went to the front desk and got something from the manager.

As he returned he held it up for the Ironman to see. "They changed our room. New one is 807. Here's the key."

Lyons nodded his understanding. He'd felt worse, but he'd sure as hell felt better. All he wanted right now were clean sheets and about twenty hours of stacking z's.

"I'm going to swing by the bar and get a bottle," said Gadgets, handing him the key. "You go on up."

"I'll wait."

"It could be a while." Gadgets gestured at the bar, which was still filled with vacationers. Numbly Lyons nodded and trudged to the elevator.

The Ironman found the room without difficulty. He started to take the usual survival precautions before entering it. Then fatigue got the better of him, and he just inserted the key and turned it.

He did, however, stand to one side, by the wall rather than in front of the door. Some habits you just never break, he thought wryly.

No gunfire or other explosive surprises greeted him.

He stepped into the darkness and found the light switch. He clicked it on as he pulled the door shut.

And then he smelled it.

A voice greeted him. It came from inside the room. It came from heaven.

"If you've still got that twenty, sailor, I'd like to pick up where we left off."

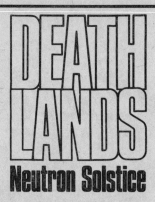

4 FREE BOOKS
1 FREE GIFT
NO RISK
NO OBLIGATION
NO KIDDING

SPECIAL LIMITED-TIME OFFER

Mail to **Gold Eagle Reader Service**

In the U.S.	In Canada
901 Fuhrmann Blvd.	P.O. Box 603,
P.O. Box 1394	Fort Erie, Ont.
Buffalo, N.Y. 14240-1394	L2A 5X3

YEAH! Rush me 4 free Gold Eagle novels and my free mystery bonus. Then send me 6 brand-new novels every other month as they come off the presses. Bill me at the low price of just $14.95— a 13% saving off the retail price. There are no shipping, handling or other hidden costs. There is no minimum number of books I must buy. I can always return a shipment and cancel at any time. Even if I never buy another book from Gold Eagle, the 4 free novels and the mystery bonus are mine to keep forever.   166–BPM–BPF6

_____
Name   (PLEASE PRINT)

_____
Address   Apt. No.

_____
City   State/Prov.   Zip/Postal Code

_____
Signature (If under 18, parent or guardian must sign)

This offer is limited to one order per household and not valid to present subscribers. Price is subject to change.

                                        NO–SUB–IA